Nicboth

The Journey Begins

Cleve Sylcox

PublishAmerica
Baltimore

© 2007 by Cleve Sylcox.
All rights reserved. No part of this book may be reproduced, stored in a retrieval system or transmitted in any form or by any means without the prior written permission of the publishers, except by a reviewer who may quote brief passages in a review to be printed in a newspaper, magazine or journal.

First printing

All characters in this book are fictitious, and any resemblance to real persons, living or dead, is coincidental.

At the specific preference of the author, PublishAmerica allowed this work to remain exactly as the author intended, verbatim, without editorial input.

ISBN: 1-4241-9320-6
PUBLISHED BY PUBLISHAMERICA, LLLP
www.publishamerica.com
Baltimore

Printed in the United States of America

Acknowledments

I would like to thank Kyle, my youngest son. He contributed greatly to the story flow, and editing as our thoughts flowed into keystrokes. This story is as much his as it is mine. Special thanks to my wife Suzanne who patiently critiqued my work, and to my oldest son, Joshua who told me to never stop dreaming.

Prologue

Nazi Germany, Berlin

"Jews...what good are they. They come into our country multiplying like rats, then they open businesses and shops stealing the income away from the hard working German people, they must be eliminated," unknown German citizen.

This is a dark time in the world.

A nation thinks their race is better than another; a country feels they must have what another country posses or even worse, when a country tries to take over the world.

Hitler has the German populace feeling supreme over all nationalities; they are the ultimate race, better in every way.

The Germans demonstrate this imagined authority by taking over Poland, Austria and most of Europe. They invade Russia, North Africa and bomb England mercilessly.

Systematically, they subject the Jews to genocide, while the German people go about their daily affairs, some knowing, some suspecting, but none saying a word.

Those who suspect keep quiet. Those who know say nothing. They chance losing all they own and maybe sentenced to death.

During the later days of the war, 1945, a few speak out against

Hitler and his felonious acts. Most are arrested. Some sent to concentration camps, others hung. However, seven of them remain in German prisons in the heart of Berlin.

These seven began the war in various high ranks of the German political machine. Toward the end of the war had enough of the murder and blood shed. They began speaking out against the brutal German government.

With the Americans and Russians closing in on Berlin, and with Hitler's smoldering remains barely cooled, the German Generals order these seven executed. They know too much of the past—too much of a liability to be left alive.

Guards escort these seven into the bombed city where once stood a mighty fortress of tall buildings containing art, and culture. This is where the German population once cheered their little corporal. One by one the guards shoot the prisoners in back of the head.

One of the seven clutches a confession he wrote a few hours before the guards escorted them onto the heap of rocks. In it, he admits his guilt…his betrayal to the world. The letter tells of how it all started. How he wishes he had told the truth in the beginning.

This is more than a confession; it's his warning to the world. The demons which control his country will not stop until they have the earth under their command.

As he hears the German officer's footsteps stop behind him, time seems to slow down, as every nuance of movement becomes slow sequences in time. All sound seems amplified absorbing his conscious.

He feels the barrel press on the back of his neck at the base of his skull. A flock of black birds takes flight before him. The wind rustles leaves. His own breath sounds intense. As he exhales, squeezing the paper tightly in his fist, the shot blisters through his skull.

He falls helpless to the rocky debris at his feet.

Rain begins to fall as a motor shell explodes a few yards away casting rocks and cinders in all directions. The Germans sprint to escape the allies advance leaving the seven where they fell.

Russia arrives first, into the heart of the shelled city finding many German papers, books, and other documents holding secrets to weapons not yet built and some in the process. They also find Hitler's carcass—smoldering in a shallow pit.

As the Americans and British push into Berlin they find the camps, graves, records of those in the camps, and hear stories from the survivors. They see German soldiers hanging from gallows with signs around their necks condemning them as traitors.

They also find books, papers containing military secrets. They also find one more thing...a letter of confession.

A GI finds the letter turning it over to his Lieutenant. Eventually, the letter makes it to Washington D.C... It is placed under lock and key—hidden away.

The Americans find this letter disturbing, yet for some reason hide it away. The government never reveals it to the public, not even to their own citizens. As some it seems, want the power as well.

The trails following the war convict some high ranking German officers to death, others to prison for life. However, none of the convicted reveals the main cause for the war. They are afraid, rightfully so. The demons that watch them will not let them be at peace, not even after death.

After the war, America becomes the world's warrior, soon becoming its lender, construction contractor, defender, and lawmaker. The world watches as the Americans drop two Atomic bombs on Japan, then holds their breath for forty years while Russia and the U.S. compete in the Cold War.

The new Millennium finds America as the only true world power. Russia is reeling in the wake of economic problems, as the rest of the world struggles in old traditional blights. Only time will tell how these past events paint the new millennium, when maybe the truth is finally set free.
This is a story about such a time.
A time of decisions followed by indecision,
A time of spiritual strength and weakness,
A time of drawing near, and drifting apart,
….A time of angels, and demons.

To those who like fantasy mixed with reality.

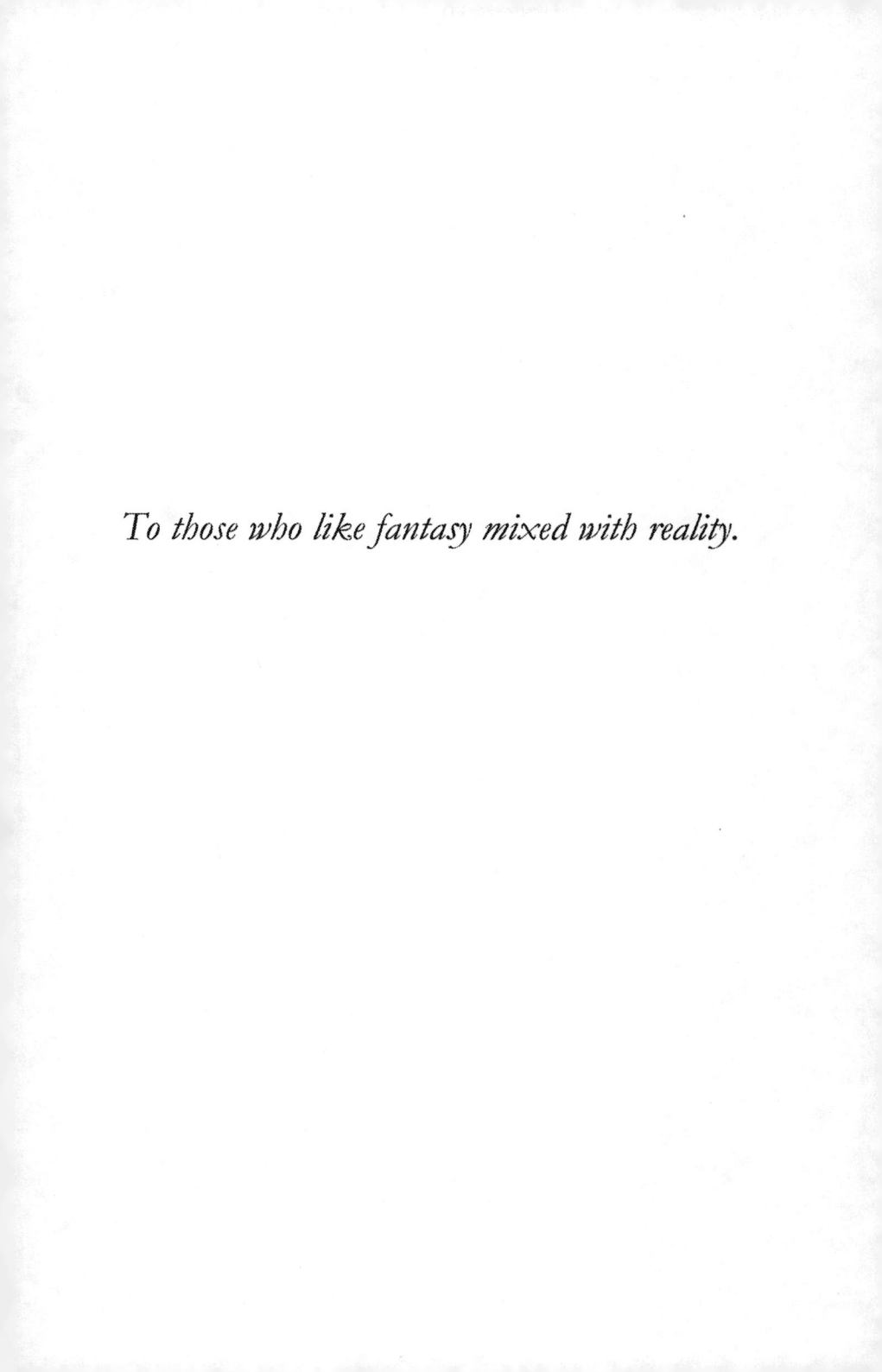

Chapter 1
Que

Present Day in an Office in Washington, D.C.
"The people are at a point where they have no clear choice for leadership. Both parties seem so much a like…no one can tell the difference. Sure, they have other parties to choose from, but they're either too far to the left or right for most citizens to stomach. It's time for a new party," the Congressman slams his fat fist on the conference table rattling pens and glasses of water.

He continues, "One that will encompass the people's desires, while maintaining a preservation of the government that gives us our freedom," shouts Congressman Ralph Syms.

His large stature, along with his pronounced stomach, looms over the oval oak conference table where four Senators and six lawyers sit listening to Syms every word. Sweat beads on Syms forehead. His face turns a light shade of red as his teeth grip tightly to a cigar stub.

His audience sits attentive with their hands folded on the tabletop staring straight at Syms.

Most find Syms offensive, at first, however, his abrasive and sharp anger seems to attract people. His constituents keep him a step ahead of his opponents in every election. They move his bills through Congress and the Senate with little or no resistance.

The four Senators are Syms right hand keeping him informed of the, goings on, on Capitol Hill. In the past they took part in his schemes to over throw other parties, rigging voting booths, losing ballots, and threatening opponents. They will do anything for him.

The four sit wondering about the Lawyers.

"The country is ripe," he continues, "...the votes are divided, split right down the middle. This proves the people are confused. One candidate isn't any better that the other. That isn't what America wants! They want choice! They want to choose between steak, and hamburger, not between chocolate and vanilla ice cream! I'm telling all of you the time is now! Now, is the time to propagate! Now, is the time! The Frontier is out there gentleman. The hearts of the American people are ripe for a new brand of leadership!"

He slams his fist to the table. The violent action shakes his jowls flinging sweat into the air. It lands on the smooth table beading into small pools. The corners of his mouth foam white from the build up of saliva, while the smell of perspiration reeks from his sweat-laden body. Wiping his face with a handkerchief, he sits down exhausted.

The ten sit anxiously waiting his next words. Never before has the Congressman shown such fury. They now watch as Syms begins to lean forward, suddenly gasping for air. His large frame twist as his face turns a deep red. With his hands grasping at his chest he turns quickly to the right falling onto his back.

The four Senators spring from their chairs to his aid.

It is too late.

Senator Newton raises his head from Syms chest where his

ears fail to hear a heart beat. The man with the vision is gone. Newton stands looking down at the man he thought would lead them into the New Age. Then he turns to speak to the lawyers, but the lawyers are gone.

That night, the Senators huddle together in a diner drinking coffee. No one is speaking as their minds race with unanswered questions about the lawyers, Syms, and their future. Unknown to them, an invisible force is watching their every move.

"They seem lost," Giggles Python, a small, thin lizard like demon, "...I wonder which one Que will pick?"

"I know," sneers Lapo. Another demon shaped like a toad, "...but you will have to wait to find out," he deeply bellows.

Python finds none of this to his liking. This fat slob of a demon knowing more than he does, he will have none of that. Besides, he knows Lapo is a spy. Python quietly uncoils his six-inch long claws. In a flash the nails plunge deep into Lapo causing the toad to arch his back, screeching with pain. Puffs of green smoke exit from the wounds. Instantly Lapo disappears in a cloud of green mist, and is no more.

"You might know, but now you will never tell," Python giggles as he moves closer to the four Senators.

Invisible, Python sits in the middle of the table looking at the Senators faces. He enjoys watching them whimper.

"Which one will Que pick," Python ask Bel, a tall, powerful demon General.

"The choice is clear Python. Which one would you pick," growls Bel.

"Who am I to choose such a worthy human? I hate them, I hate them all! However, if I had to pick one I would choose him," Python points to Senator Drake, "He seems to have some intelligence. Maybe he will do our deeds nicely," Python giggles, "I do hold the choice...Don't I?"

Bel turns his back to Python grunting softly, "Yes, he is the one," Bel answers to satisfy Python, but he really does not know, "Now go! Spread the word. The time is now! Gather our forces together at Nicboth. Make sure they post guards. I don't want Michael ruining this like he did last time."

Python sits in the center of the table spinning in circles sticking his tongue out at the humans.

"Go," shouts Bel.

Python leaps to the air, taking wing into the night. Hundreds of demons surround the four Senators leering down on them.

Bel is suddenly still. He raises his hand over his head, "Que's here," he shouts.

The army and Bel, kneel to an invisible force that controls them, feeds them, directing even their thoughts with the slightest of ease. As Bel and his forces are invisible to humans, Que is invisible to common demons. The diner fills with smoke only the demons can see, causing the demons to tremble. Above one of the Senators heads appears a glowing ball of fire. It spins rapidly until bursting sending sparks flying in all directions.

The diners' lights flicker, then go out.

Bel watches, as above the head of the same Senator appears a single glowing red orb. Bel knows he is the one Que demands to replace Syms.

When the diners' lights flicker back on, one Senator is missing.

* * *

Sharon looks up at a deep blue sky. A slight breeze begins to blow her long black hair lightly about on her shoulders.

Bold thunderheads fill the far horizon. She knows the towns to her south are in for another hard night of rain. Heavy down pours is just more water on top of already swollen ponds, lakes, creeks and rivers.

Sharon is an expert Meteorologist, from the Melbourne Institute of Climatic Weather. They sent her to America's heartland at the request from the United States NWS (National Weather Service) to investigate an unusual weather pattern. The U.S. sent request all over the world in an attempt to gather the best minds in the field. Most requests went unanswered, as the countries of the Northern Hemisphere are much too busy reacting to their own weather problems. The Southern Hemisphere, however, seems immune to these strange changes. Sharon doesn't worry about the rest of the world, as she has her own problems.

A large massive low-pressure area formed in the Pacific cutting off the Jet Stream to the Central region of the United States. This anomaly causes stationary weather pockets, which seem to float in a larger pocket of hot stagnant air. Some areas remain dry, while others have an over abundance of rain. Moisture trapped in this dome slowly rotates in the pocket. It always brings the same results, massive flooding in some areas, while others remain dry.

Sharon studied all the raw data from the computers then looking through every meteorological book she finds, but nothing like this is on record lasting for such an extended duration. Three months passed, still no relief in sight, bridges washed away in one county, while just over the county line grass fires are commonplace.

Torrents of rain explode from the sky sweeping away everything in its path. She has seen this torrent from a distance. It looks like a wall of water moving across the countryside, as it is miles wide and several miles deep. The roar of the wind and rain thunders across the land as lighting crackles in the billowing cumulous clouds stretching high above.

She wants to get closer…close enough to feel the roar, feel the mist from the rain. She hops into her Jeep driving towards the thunderheads, the county line, and her destiny.

Chapter 2
The Impending Storm

    Shadows grow long at Wilbur Lake as the sun sets on the far horizon beyond the lakes low rolling hills. As the sun sinks below the hills, twilight cascades the sky with red, yellow, and blue hues, creating a wide array of colors. One by one the stars appear in the darkening sky.

    The sun finishes its journey of the day relinquishing its kingdom to the stars which now fill the sky. The heat of the day remains in a stale vacuum, the air is still, sticky…stuffy.

    Darkness blankets the woods surrounding the lake creating a black ridge above the ever-increasing shoreline. The exposed shoreline wraps a ribbon of gray around the small lake at night as the full moon shines brightly against its white sand and rock.

    Charles Hanson sits in his old rowboat fishing for catfish, while behind him in the distance thunder rumbles. He finds this serene laying his fishing rod down in the boat, leaning back across the boats center support looking up at the stars. He is alone on the lake as no one visits here anymore. Many prefer to go elsewhere than be trapped out here if it should rain. Charles lives nearby and sees no sense worrying about such matters.

It is getting late. He decides that he better get home before his wife misses him. He picks up the ores turning the boat toward his truck. As the boat turns he looks up over the hillside where he can see the flashes of lightning from behind the hills in the distance. He wonders why the storm never moves from Warren County.

"Must be God," he mutters to himself.

Many nights he sat on his back porch watching storms move in from the west, but now the storms never move. He relishes the thought of when it rains again.

The old metal boat scrapes against the rocks as it slides to a halt on shore. Charles pulls the boat up the bank to a tree where he wraps a chain through the loop of its metal tongue before securing it with a lock. He tugs the chain a few times then lets it fall to the dusty ground in a heap. He stands watching the lightning, and listening to the thunder.

"Interesting, that lightning," he thinks, "…seems to be jumping sideways."

He climbs into his truck starting its motor. Slamming his squeaky truck door he puts the truck in gear, and accelerates. Before long his taillights are rounding a far bend of the dusty road, disappearing in the haze of night.

The lake is left to the occasional croak of a frog and the chirping of crickets. Lightning reflects off the lakes still surface; shimmers of light bounce into the woods, while the frogs and crickets become still ending their recital.

A gentle breeze rocks a dried leaf, as the sky rolls out a sheet of clouds to cover the stars. The wind gust, creating a roar of clattering leaves as the wind passes through the woods leaving an eerie silence in its wake.

Lighting cracks across the sky, thunder explodes, clouds grow thick as they roll above the lake. The wind charges down from the Heavens racing through the woods swirling leaves and cracking limbs.

The clouds open sending torrents of rain splashing to the ground sliding Charles boat side-ways, breaking the chains and tossing it into the now churning lake. The woods become a chatterbox of crackling leaves as wind forced rain tears through them. Pools of water form flowing together turning into streams. Violent rivers emerge from the surrounding hillsides carrying run-off into the lake. The lake level lurches upward, and soon is more than the spillway can carry.

The pressure is too much for the earthen dam gives birth.

* * *

Sharon stands on a hill at the Lincoln County line looking into the darkness. Lightning flashes in front of her as rain pours down a few feet away. The only moisture she feels is the occasional mist blown by the wind. She is amazed at what she is witnessing. The headlights from her Jeep reveal a wall of water coming straight down.

She looks down the hill at the runoff. She can hear the raging water below her beyond the reach of the headlights. Her investigative instincts compel her to go into the rain, but something is holding her back. She knows this could be dangerous especially at night and all alone. Instead she hurries to her Jeep, gets her camera taking pictures. She then runs back to the jeep getting her video camera. As she films her Aussie voice details the event.

"This is the, 'Wall,'" she pans the rain and moves closer, "I don't know if you can hear me well with the noise from the rain, just look at this," She exclaims, "Isn't this incredible. I hope this comes across to you as well as I'm seeing it here."

She moves toward the down sloop of the hill, "Incredible, incredible! Look at this…"

She stops the camera running back to the Jeep. Reaching under the driver's seat she finds a paper cup, then runs towards the wall. She holds the camera out in front of her pointing it towards herself. She clicks the camera on.

"I will now prove the stories are true. I will now get a drink of rain," She holds the camera tightly with her left hand, while holding the cup in her right. Extending her right arm out, she sticks the cup into the wall. The force of the rain strikes her hand with such intensity she nearly falls over, almost loosing her grip on the camera. When she pulls the cup out it is crinkled.

"As you can see the cup is almost gone, but I'm still able to drink from it," she raises the torn cup to her lips drinking the rain. She looks straight into the camera and smiles. Clicking off the camera she now rushes back to the Jeep,

"I have to get this to the guys," she says as she climbs behind the wheel.

She drives quickly down the twisting dirt road, stopping at the top of a hill near the main asphalt road that leads back to her hotel. From here she is facing almost directly at the storm miles away. She notices something different; "It's moving," Sharon pulls the video-camera up to her eye. Through the viewfinder she watches and records this massive movement of lightning, thunder, and rain.

* * *

Blackness surrounds Senator Newton as he stumbles to his feet. Cold dampness grips him as he begins to shiver. His nice suit, soiled, stained from the mud of the cave. His eyes search desperately for any light. His hands probe the darkness to touch anything that might give him a clue of his surroundings.

He finds the wall of the cave feeling the rough, damp rock, "Where in the World... Someone must have slipped me something...The lights...the lights in the diner went out, yes, and now I'm here, but how.... someone knocked me out and put me here, but my head doesn't hurt...drugs, yes, then it must have been drugs."

The Senator nervously tries to find some explanation, "I'm dreaming...or something like that. It has to be a nightmare of sorts..."

"This is no nightmare Senator. It is the start of the greatest opportunity you've ever encountered," Bel announces.

The Senator staggers backwards, falling hard on his right side. All thoughts of dreaming quickly flee from his mind.

"Who's there, and what do you want with me," Newton wrestles himself to his feet standing defiant to this disembodied voice.

Bel smiles as he ignites a fire on the ground behind Newton.

The Senator turns quickly to the flame, frantically looking around. The flame reveals the rough vast interior of the cave. Large rocks and huge stalagmites dwarf him.

"Does that make you feel better? Being able to see, or does it frighten you Senator," Bel laughs loudly sending his eerie cackle echoing throughout the cavity. Bel's army follows their leader joining in the laughter creating a variety of screeching and cackling.

Newton begins to shake with fear as he covers his ears, dropping to his knees.

"Ah, that's more like it. It is good to see you on your knees," Bel taunts.

"Why have you brought me here, and who are you...the Devil," Newton shouts.

"Oh, no, not me, I'm just here to give you a message from one who sits on high," Bels voice takes on a more somber tone, "He wants you to know him as your friend, as your father," Bel smiles at his artistry of deceit.

"Do you mean God," the Senator asks. He was never a believer and doesn't know a thing about the Bible. Bel knows this.

"Yes, now sit down," Bel commands.

Newton sits down wearily on top of a large flat rock. His thoughts are confused, which gives Bel the upper hand.

Python sits on a large boulder in front of Newton grinning.

"Let's see," Bel begins, "…he wants you to help him. I know he doesn't need help from anyone, and I'm sure you know that, but there are those that are doing everything they can to interfere with his efforts," Bel's voice is soft and steady.

"You've seen this I'm sure. In the Middle East he wants the Jews out. Ever since they betrayed him and he cast them out into the world, he's been trying to destroy them. Hitler was working for us. Gods plan was revealed to him, just like it will be revealed to you," Bel wants to root this deceit deep into Newton, "…We not only want the Jews, but the Christians. You see, they are not really worshiping God, but their selfish needs. This will all be explained to you in more detail shortly, in the meantime sit back and relax. Soon, you will meet Que. Que is the master next to God. He will teach you everything. Remember, we chose you Senator for a purpose higher than any calling you have ever been chosen for before."

Bel motions for Python, and then becomes quiet. Something is wrong elsewhere and he must tend to it quickly. He closes his eyes tilting his head up listening to the silent commands of Que. Bel opens his eyes pointing to Python.

"Sharon Lombardy has some pictures we must retrieve. Send Roman, and two Imps," Bel commands Python.

Python takes flight into the dark confines of the cave.

Newton leans back on the rock stunned, "You mean all those

people going to church, and those claiming to worship God are misled," Newton drags his fingers through his hair.

"Yes, and refuse to join us, because they are so deceived," Bel begins to speak, and then stops. He feels Que nearby.

The floor of the cave begins to tremble as the walls turn a dark red as the vibrations subside, then the walls return to their natural color.

Newton stands looking around, "What are you doing, what is going on," he stammers.

"Sit down," Que's deep voice echoes in the chamber.

Newton covers his ears while backing to a boulder. He sits nervously facing the direction of the voice. His breath is quick, and his pulse is fast. Never in his life has he experienced such confusion, and thinks he is going mad.

"Don't speak," Bel warns Newton, "Just sit and look into the flame."

Newton turns his head to the flame behind him. Dancing in the flame he sees different colors of light dancing around each other. Transfixed he continues to stare at the flame. His legs grow numb, while his arms become limp. He falls into a trance with his eyes glued on the colors. He is completely oblivious to everything.

Smoke slowly swirls above his head. Like a snake it coils around his cranium, probing his nostrils before entering his nose. There is nothing the Senator can do. Que speaks directly to the marrow of Newton's mind. At the same instance the colors reshape themselves into visual images of what Que is saying to him.

*   *   *

"Listen, what do you mean…what…I can't hear you," Sharon tries to speak to her colleague Bruce Wilson at the Wies Suites Conservatory in Sidney, Australia as she drives toward her hotel. Static crackles on her cell phone.

"The atmosphere...nothing...changed," Bruce's voice is interrupted repeatedly by static.

Sharon listens trying to piece together what he is saying.

"...cell is moving into...you're needed...send quickly," more static interrupts Bruce.

"Bruce, listen. I took some pictures and will send them to you via email, and I got some tape I will send you Fed Express, got that, Bruce...Bruce?"

"Yes, I got most of that. Did you...about the cell," Bruce answers.

"Yes, but what direction is it moving?"

"Right then...moving east.... toward you," Bruce warns. "...it's moving into a different location, different..."

"Oh! Bruce...Bruce...darn phone, Bruce if you can here me I have to go."

Sharon listens for a reply, there is none. She pulls into her motel parking lot grabbing her laptop case, then hurrying through the door leading into the lobby. Approaching the elevator the lights in the lobby begin to flicker, then go out.

"Stop her! Don't let her send those pictures," Roman yells.

Roman sends two Imps from the power pole transformer to the lobby.

They circle Sharon whispering into her ear, "You're not going to send anything. You're all alone, and no one can help you now."

As they whisper Sharon feels a cold chill come over her. Goose bumps run tracks up her spine, and down her arms. Her heart races, her mind fill's with illusions of isolation.

"Leave! Go back home. Who would blame you for quitting now," the two whisper.

Sharon wants to walk forward, but feels trapped.

"This whole assignment is more than you bargained for. Just leave now before it is too late," the two continue.

Sharon looks to her right seeing the doorway leading to the

stairwell. From there she can walk up three flights to her floor, then to her room. She now feels sick to her stomach. Her joints ache, and she has a headache.

"You must not rest until you leave…there's time to sleep on the plane. Go to your room and pack," the imps taunt.

Sharon feels dizzy as the room spins around her. Then she hears another voice. It is softer than the other two.

"It's ok Sharon. You're not alone. We are here," softly the deep voice assures.

The two Imps look in front of Sharon and see a man dressed in a long white robe. His hair is like sunshine. A bright light shines all around him.

"You! Move and get out of her way Michlu before we cut you to shards," the two demand looking around for Roman. They know they don't stand a chance against Michlu…he is Michael's General.

"Be gone," shouts Michlu at the same time he raises his arms above his head. The two tumble backward through the lobby doors into the darkness of night.

Sharon staggers a bit suddenly feeling much better. The lights flicker back on as the elevator door opens. Wasting no time she runs to the elevator.

Reaching her floor she rushes into her room falling exhausted on the bed.

Looking out her window like a watchman guarding against attack is Michlu.

* * *

Charles Hanson pulls his truck into his long rock driveway leading to his old farmhouse. He inherited two-hundred acres of prime pasture from his father. Like his father he uses it to raise his own stock of bulls. That was until age caught up with him. He finds a steadier income in renting most of the pasture to other farmers. At his age renting and letting others do most of the work is a lot easier than doing the work himself, but that might end if rain doesn't come soon.

The pasture is usually full of prime hoofed beef. Now, the land is empty, and the grass is brown. His beef long since sold off, as Charles wanted to make his money before the drought melted away his profits. The renters moved their cattle further south where the weather is more stable. The ponds and his wells are dry. He doesn't have any farm animals left to worry about. His cat finds enough mice to eat in the barn. His wife, Charlotte, is his only concern.

Both are well into their seventy's, and she's been sick lately. He doesn't understand her obsession with the Bible, and all this talk she gives him about being saved. He shakes his head just thinking about it.

"Crazy talk, that's all it is, just plain crazy," he mumbles.

The porch light is on. The old farmhouse is a welcome sight. Parking the truck along side his white picket fence he hurries to the house while looking at the night sky behind him. The stars quickly disappear as the storm makes it way toward him.

"Finally, the rain is coming," he says out loud.

It is to late this season to recapture the lushness of his pasture, but if he gets the rain now the pasture could recover by early spring.

Entering the house, he finds Charlotte sleeping on the coach. A ceiling fan squeaks as it turns above her. The hot sticky air of the house surrounds Charles. He wakes Charlotte who is soaked to the skin in sweat. He helps her to the back porch to find relief from the heat.

The air is still. In the distance they can see the lighting, and hear the thunder. He helps her sit down in her rocker then brings her a cool glass of water. He sits in his rocker next to her. Holding Charlotte's hand he pats it as they sit rocking.

"The rain is coming dear, and our pasture will be better than ever, you'll see," Charles tries to assure her.

Charlotte rocks with her head resting against the high headboard of the rocker. She rocks slowly and silently, with her eyes steadily looking ahead.

Charles is worried about her. The air conditioning went out about a month ago. Since then they've had to sleep on cots on the porch. She needs a soft bed and air-conditioning. The heat in the house is just unbearable.

"Damn service techs," Charles thinks aloud as he stairs at the air-conditioner cooling unit next to the house, "Afraid of a little rain, pft."

Charlotte's eyes close. Her rocking stops as she falls asleep. He thinks about moving her to the nearby cots, but decides to let her rest and sit back to watch the rain.

He does not have a television, or own a radio. The radio in the truck broke years ago. He hasn't spoken with his neighbors for sometime. He thinks how weird they are anyway with all that, "Christian junk."

He ponders his solitude for a moment, "Isolated…like the man on the moon," he sits waiting for a nice summer thundershower.

Above his head is a wind chime made out of tin horses, and tin cowboys. In front of him is a large oak tree. It towers above their two-story farmhouse. It is as wide as the front of his truck. Hanging from its limbs is eight more wind chimes of varying types. Charles wonders when the last time he heard any of them make a sound. A slight breeze blows swaying all the chimes to life, clanging slightly then fading.

Charles looks up and smiles, "Here it comes," he sits on the edge of the rocker with his elbows on his knees leaning forward looking into the sky through the limbs of the Oak.

Fast moving clouds cover the stars. The thunder becomes louder, as the lighting strikes closer the chimes burst into concert.

Charles wakes Charlotte. "Honey, now come on, we have to go inside. I think this is definitely goanna be a drought buster."

He hurries Charlotte into the house sitting her on a chair in the hallway, "Now you stay right there. I don't want you to get hurt," Charlotte looks up at him and smiles.

After kissing her he returns to the back porch.

The sky is black as sackcloths.

The wind blows in a gale bending the Oaks limbs. Charles can hear the limbs scarp against his roof.

The storm grabs the chimes casting them into the gloom. The house creeks, and moans as the wind pushes hard against it.

The gale suddenly increases forcing Charles into the house. He watches horrified as the oak's limbs snap sailing over the house and into obscurity...then a low roar. The roar grows loader, and is soon deafening. Thinking it is a tornado; Charles retreats to the safety of the hall only to find an empty chair where Charlotte once sat.

"Charlotte," Charles yells.

His voice is barely audible above the roar. He runs back to the porch, then to the front of the house. There he sees her walking towards the barn struggling to stay on her feet against the gale.

"Charlotte," Charles continues to yell.

He rushes out the front door only to be blown down onto the muddy barnyard. He struggles to his feet, but the blast of air is too much. He lay on the ground yelling for Charlotte to come back. He looks behind him just in time to see the wall of water before it engulfs him.

Charlotte reaches the barn door. She struggles to open the

heavy door as the wind pushes against it. She can hear the howls riding on the current as white ghostly figures waft past her. She knows the source of their evilness. She says a prayer then pulls on the door with all her might. The door opens enough for her to squeeze through just as the wall reaches her. The barn sways, creeks, and moans as the pounding torrents of rain plunge down on the old red structure striking hard against the tin roof. The gale lifts the tin, slamming it down, while rain pounds on the wooden walls. Charlotte finds an old corncrib filed with straw, and crawls into it. The gale is relentless, swaying the building even harder. The structure rocks back and fourth until finally the red walls fall…the tin roof collapse.

CHAPTER 3
The Gathering

Fragmented memories of a night better off forgotten fill Newton's mind as he tosses under his covers. Last night is a blur, a sweeping flight of fancy which he cannot recall. Opening his eyes looking toward the window he can see the sun is barely over the horizon. He never gets up before seven, but yet he is fully awake.

He tosses back onto his side wrapping himself in the covers hoping to resume his slumber. The effort is useless as his mind runs uncontrolled with thoughts he never had before. After several minutes he gives up. Walking into the restroom he finds his clothes scattered everywhere. His muddy pants hung haphazardly on the shower rod. His soiled shirt piled on top of his muddy shoes. His socks lay in the sink. Mud smeared all over the floor, sink, tub and toilet.

"What in the world," he wonders as he runs his fingers through his hair.

Pic and Dome, two demons, fly around the senator's head.

"You're the one Que has chosen...remember," whispers Pic.

"Quickly, you have so much to do," whispers Dome.

Newton listens to the disembodied voices...he remembers. A new consciousness awakens inside of him. His thoughts flow effortlessly into an understanding of his new being.

"Yes, I...I do remember now. A cave and a fire with colors swirling around...Yes, I do remember," Newton looks into the mirror and deep into the reflection of his eyes. Shining back at him are the hands of souls reaching out of his iris then plunging deep into the blackness of his pupil, "You're the chosen one," he says to himself, then smiles.

The night in the cave rushes to the forefront of his mind, although twisted, he believes he is working for God. Que's deception works wonderfully...Newton is now his puppet.

In Newton's mind colors swirl. In his head, voices whisper. Small, almost microscopic red demons called, Derties, crawl out of the pours of his ear lobe. They whisper into his ear Que's instructions to take over Congress and the Senate. However, Newton's mind is distracted by all the new thoughts overwhelming him. He hears, but does not listen.

Newton cleans up the mess in the bath, takes a shower and gets dressed, then calls the three Senators that were with him at Syms meeting. As he opens the front door to leave he finds the six lawyers standing on his front porch.

"We're glad you made it Senator. You do remember us from yesterday?" Bill Taylor speaks for all six of them. "We are at your service. I'm Bill Taylor. You..."

"You don't have to tell me who you are," Newton interrupts, "...I already know who all of you are. Syms was too reckless, and as you saw yesterday not ready for this task. We will take over Washington D.C., Gentlemen...follow me."

The lawyers smile as they move to the side to allow their new leader past.

Ce and Dome know the six lawyers too; they brought the six to Que.

* * *

Bruce Wilson looks at the latest readings on his monitor. He is at the Meteorological Observatory in Sydney, "This is raw data Ben. We can't be sure of anything until we let the computers run it."

Ben Gameberlin is the head of meteorological studies for Melbourne Institute of Climatic Weather, Sharon's employer and Bruce's boss. Ben is trying to persuade Bruce that the cell in the Pacific is growing larger.

"Sure I agree," Bruce, continues, "the cell has increased two fold according to these numbers and appears to be gaining strength, but if you aren't positive of where it's going or what it's doing we could place millions of people in a panic needlessly. I'm just asking for us to be sure."

"What evidence do you need, Bruce? The Central regions of the U.S. are a swamp, and other parts are practically deserts. The whole world is facing diverse weather patterns; Asia hasn't had it's usual monsoons, Europe is frozen solid by irregular winter snows, heavier than normal snows in Canada and Russia, the regions around the equator have temperatures in the mid 80's, and this cell is to blame for them all! If this cell moves one degree in any direction with the amount of force it's gaining the Americas could get washed away, Europe will be one big ball of ice and God only knows what will happen to the rest of the world," Ben's anger grows, "...and if you think you know it all then set on those reports for the next hour while that monster in the Pacific grows larger," Ben stands leaning on his desk while yelling, "Now get with it!"

"Alright, alright I'll call the U.S. Weather Service and fax them our report, and then I'll call Sharon to see if she's alright," Bruce turns reluctantly to the reports on his monitor before picking up the phone, "Crazy, simply crazy," he mutters.

Ben knows Bruce is not very experienced, and tolerates Bruce's question most of the time, but this is not the time for questions, it is a time for action.

"Sharon better be in that hotel, and don't tell me if she's out in that stuff gathering information. She should be on a plane back here," Ben shouts across his desk to Bruce, who waves one hand in the air and nods his head.

Ben worries a lot about Sharon and her habits of recklessness. He's been reporting meteorological information to the Australian population for twenty years, ten of those years to the Australian Military, never has he had anyone in his employment like her; she carelessly explores dangerous situations—caution is not in her vocabulary.

Ben is a seasoned veteran of hurricanes, and all kinds of diverse weather. He is tall, skinny and walks leaning slightly to the right from an old injury that he refuses to talk about. He is only in his early forties, but his premature gray hair makes him appear much older.

This is in contrast to Bruce. Bruce is a fine looking young man fresh out of college; graduated with honors, first in his class, star football player, but working for Ben is his first real job in the meteorological arena.

"Did you call Sharon yet," Ben barks from under his desk, "There it is. If I don't loose more pens under here…Bruce! Did you call her?"

"I'm doing it know," Bruce shouts without looking away from his monitor.

* * *

Sharon sits in her hotel room looking over the photos on her laptop. She usually does not take pictures well, but these look sharp, focused. Attaching the photos to an email to send to Bruce does not take her but a few seconds, sending them even less. Retrieving her morning cup of coffee she left next to the bed across the room a feeling comes over her as if she is missing something, something she overlooked, or didn't catch in those digital images she sent.

Sharon picks up her coffee as she stands across the room staring out the hotel window. Swirling the rim of the cup with her finger she turns gazing at the graphic on the laptop monitor.

"What could it be? It's just a lot of water, nothing…hmm, maybe a shape," She thinks out loud.

Hurrying across the room to the laptop she opens a graphic program to help her analyze the picture. Opening the first picture she sees the front fender of the Jeep, past that is the slopping hill. Moving still further is a direct line dividing the photo in half. Everything above that line is rain pouring down to the line where the rain gathers and runs down the hill away from the Jeep, "It looks like a waterfall…. just water."

As she sips the last of her coffee her eyes examines every detail of the image, still nothing pops out as different. Walking across the room she picks up the coffeepot to refill the cup, when she sees it.

"Oh my," she exclaims almost dropping her cup.

Wide eyed, Sharon stares intently at the laptop screen. Her steps are slow as her mind tries to rationalize the image within the image. As she reaches the table she lightly moves her fingers across the image of a bearded man. The face is familiar to her. Something moves inside her. She doesn't understand what it is, but she feels this is important. She opens another picture.

In this picture she sees a close up of the wall. The image is there and more detailed. The mouth appears to be open.

She moves across the room and looks back at the screen. The face is very familiar.

Opening another picture she sees the Jeeps right fender, the slopping hill, and then the wall. Sharon drops her coffee cup to the floor, and covers her mouth. The image now shows the man with his hands extended toward her and his mouth is definitely open. She does not believe what she is seeing.

Michlu tips over the video-camera case.

She turns toward the noise then walks over to the bag, kneeling next to it.

"That's funny, how in the world," then she remembers the recording.

She connects the camera to the laptop then begins playing the tape.

Her voice is loud above the noise of the rain, as she watches the water pouring down from the sky. In the wall she sees the same image she saw in the photos. It is definitely a breaded face and his lips do seem to be moving. Above his head she can see another faded image with wings, but not as detailed. The scene changes to her drinking the rain, then the footage ends with her smiling at the camera.

Rewinding the scene, she plays this over several times using the programs editing functions to increase the background noise producing a grabbled deep voice. This stimulates her curiosity. She plugs in her headphones listening carefully, but is unable to determine any clear words or phrases. Exhausting all the programs resources to isolate and sharpen the deep tones she determines a more sophisticated program is required to get her desired results, she gives up.

Her cell phone rings. She hops out of her chair rushing to the dresser where the phone is busy ringing again. As she picks it up she hears something behind her. A low bellowing voice, much like a voice played on slow motion.

Michlu stands next to the laptop swirling his finger over the keypad.

Sharon stands holding the ringing phone listening to a clear voice of a man coming from her laptop speakers.

The voice is soft and calm, "Nicboth, you must go to Nicboth."

Slowly, she steps closer to the laptop screen. The program is still running the footage she edited. The image speaks to her while holding out his hands as he says. "…you must go…" Her heart jumps, her legs give out from under her. Falling onto the bed she can hear another voice, "We are with you," Michlu whispers in her ear.

She sits on the edge of the bed staring at the screen. The cell phone rings again. It startles her, and she drops it on the floor. She bends down to pick it up when she notices the Gideon Bible on the nightstand next to the lamp. She reaches for the book when the cell phone rings again. She answers the call with a shaky voice while opening the Bible, "Yes, this is Sharon."

"Are you a hard one to get a hold of? Where have you been," Bruce asks and is relieved she answered, but is frustrated with her at the same time.

"Oh, um I've been right here working on something very unusual. Bruce, did you get the email I sent you this morning?"

"Yes. I couldn't get you on this blasted thing, so I checked to see if you sent anything. Those pictures are amazing! How close were you to that?"

"Did you see anything different? Like an image or something?"

"No, just an extraordinary wall of rain isn't that enough out of ordinary? What do you see?"

"Bruce, I know this might sound crazy, but look at the wall of water from a distance, and look closely at the shadows," Sharon instructs hoping he will see the same thing.

"Ok Love, give me a minute here. All right then, I have the picture on my screen, you want me to look at it from a distance, about how far?

"I don't know…," Sharon eyeballs the distance from her laptop to the coffee pot, "…about ten feet, I guess."

"Ok, I'm about, ten or so away, now what?"

"Look at your screen…what do you see Bruce?"

"I see a picture with your Jeep fender in it, some ugly brown grass, and a bunch of water coming down out of Heaven like God busted a water pipe. What do you want me to see," Bruce asks as he is growing impatient, but with Sharon he will go the extra mile. He knows when she's serious, and she seems very serious now.

"Oh, I don't know," Sharon is reluctant to tell him about the image. She likes Bruce a lot and feels by telling him he might think she's a nut case, "I thought I saw something. If you didn't see anything then maybe I'm just losing my mind."

"Sharon, you alright? You don't sound like your old self."

"No, I'm fine really. Is Ben around?"

"Yeah, he is around here somewhere. He might be under his desk looking for a pen. Oh, that reminds me. We have some new data in this morning, and it looks like the cell is increasing, not only in size, but strength. We want you to come home."

"No," Sharon snaps, "I mean, no I don't need to come back just yet. I've been watching the storm's path and it is moving alright, but it is staying south of me, and moving to the east. I'll be fine."

"If you say so love. All I know is that thing looks dangerous to me. I see Ben now. You want to talk with him?"

"Yes, put him on. I'll talk with you later, and don't worry about me. I'll be just fine."

Bruce hands his cell phone to Ben, "Sharon, why aren't you on a plane right now, and it better be a good excuse," Ben barks.

"Ah, well you see, I found something here very interesting Ben…" Ben cuts Sharon off.

"Listen, the data indicates this thing is getting bigger than we ever imagined, so get on a plane this afternoon. Nothing can be so interesting that it keeps you there."

"No Ben, you have to listen! I found something in those photos, and also the recording from the camcorder shows this same thing. Ben, your going to think I'm crazy, but I think God is talking to me."

Sharon hears silence on the other end as Ben sits down still holding the phone to his ear.

"Ben…Ben…are you still there," Sharon wonders if she did the right thing. She had to tell him, "I didn't tell Bruce this because I thought he would think I was crazy, you have to help me."

"Yes…ah…well, what do you want me to do Sharon," Ben isn't sure what to say.

"Ben, look at the photos. Look closely at them, and then if you don't see anything I will call this whole thing off and be on the first flight back to Sydney," she pleads. Sharon wanted to be on a flight yesterday, but now only wants to understand the message from the image.

"Ok, Sharon, you have your wish. I'll look closer at those photos and call you later with what I find."

"Thanks Ben. You won't regret it," Sharon disconnects the call and returns to looking at the image.

Ben turns back to his desk, "Bruce, get those photos to my desk, pronto!"

* * *

"Gentleman, we stand on the brink of history. No longer will it be the same as the past where we let circumstance control the government, it will be a government controlling the circumstance," Senator Newton speaks to his disciples; the three Senators, and the six lawyers in their private meeting room.

"Last night I had a vision. After seeing Congressman Syms die yesterday I had to get away from everyone, it shook me so. Then last night a vision poured out of Heaven and drenched my soul with a promise of the future. Soon, there will be a new order that will engulf mankind in a new hierarchical province. A supreme master will rule it, but for this to happen we must first help lay the foundation. As you know most of it is already in place, and the next phase is beginning in Washington D.C. Syms was right. The frontier is the hearts and minds of the American people. We must assure them that our way is the only way. We must assure them that the only party out there that has it all together is our party."

His audience stands and applause. As the meeting progresses Newton details his plans. By mid-afternoon he has his Senators making phone calls to their constituents and the lawyers calling the candidates instructing them on how they might win.

"We will play the candidates against each other and then the next election will be ours," Newton retreats to a corner of the room where he prays to Que for guidance.

***

The sky over the pacific is a deep blue; the air is clear and the wind mild. On a remote tropical island Bel and his army waits for other divisions to join them.

Bel is not very excited about this union because he thinks his army can do this alone, and Jobauten will be there.

Ever since Bel lost to Michael at the crossroads of Rome in Jerusalem, Jobauten has taunted him, "Spineless," Bel thinks to himself when recalling Jobauten and his mocking.

In the distant horizon Bel sees Jobauten flying fast toward him. Jobauten rides on a cloud while sitting on a golden throne. The throne he claims came from Lucifer as a gift. On either side of him stand two guards. Kneeling in front of the throne, looking ahead, stand three archers.

"Sound the ready alarm," Bel barks to his trumpeters.

Two long blasts from the long horns signal the army to readiness. In full armament Bels army stands ready to confront Jobauten. Bel's sentries signal Jobauten is dividing his forces in three, and will approach the island from the north, south, and east. Bel sends his General to make the adjustments to his ranks, and then sends Python to deliver a message to Jobauten.

"Python, take this message to Jobauten. We do not wish a war between us at this time. Our mission is to combine our forces and wait for Que's next command. If you insist on fighting you will loose," Bel never backs down from a fight.

Python hesitates at first, and then takes wing, when Bels swings his sword at him nearly removing his head, "Go now," Bel demands.

Jobauten is weary of Bel. They usually stay far apart from each other and wonder if this, "uniting" is a trick on Bels part.

"Que would never combine our forces. Bel's army is mightier

and much large than mine, so why the merger," Jobauten hisses as he sees Python coming through the clouds. He halts his assault stopping all his forces in ready position. He has Bel surrounded, and even though outnumbered Jobauten's arrogance prevails, he feels as if he can defeat Bel.

"What do you want little one? Do you bring a peace offering from the failure," Jobauten sneers.

"I bring you a message from Bel," Python's squeaky voice replies as he lands in front of Jobautens throne.

"What does he want? Is he prepared to surrender," Jobauten smirks.

This makes Python mad, "Do I need to remind you that Bel is mightier in number and in strength? Do I need to remind you that Que choose Bel to command this army of millions, and to block the gates of Heaven?"

"Block the gates of Heaven? Is that what it's called when he allows the son of God full access to the earth? Not did he fail once, but thrice. Then he allows this, 'Holy Sprit,' to move freely between the Earth and the Heavens," Jobauten laughs while staring intently at Python.

"Hmmm, I do recall several times when Que commanded you to stop an angel from speaking with Daniel and you failed to hold him. Just one angel and you couldn't do it. Bel had to deal with millions of God's mightiest angels at the crossroads. Where were you then...? You were supposed to be guarding the tomb! You allowed two angels and the Son to escape! Do I also need to remind you that you were suppose to be looking for those disciples of his before the sprit descended on them and you failed to find them," Python says while raising an eyebrow.

"Enough," Jobauten waves his arm in front of him in anger, and glares at Python, "What is Bels message," he demands.

"He wants you to know he doesn't want a battle. Que wants us to join forces. It will take all of us to perform this great work for Que, or don't you think you're capable of following commands," Python feels two warriors approaching him from behind. Immediately he draws his claws standing poised for their attack, "Withdraw them, or they will disappear like your little spy, Lapo."

Jobauten knows the power of Pythons claws. He also cannot afford to loose another to their sting.

"Back away, and let him live…for now. Go, tell Bel that we will comply with Que's orders, but when this is over I want to settle our dispute."

Python laughs, "Oh, I will tell Bel everything Jobauten. Make your camp on the far side of the island. We don't want your forces stinking up our camps with their foul smell."

Several spears pass close to Pythons head, "Oh, your warriors are getting better. They almost hit me that time," Python takes flight only after dodging several more spears.

"Make camp there," Jobauten points towards a vacant strip of beach right next to Bel's camp, "We will see Python, who stinks up the place."

* * *

The rain finally ends in the early morning hours and the sun is barely over the horizon as Charles pulls himself from under the crawl space of the house. He immediately yells for Charlotte, "Charlotte…Charlotte."

Silence.

He lost track of her after the wall engulfed him, now he must find her. His heart races when he sees the barn. He hurries as fast as his aged body will allow toward the pile of broken lumber, and twisted metal.

"Charlotte, O' Lord if she's in there let her be alive," his pace is quick and the large beams of lumber seem light in his hands as he tosses one after the other from the fallen entrance to the barn, "Charlotte...Charlotte," he yells over and over again.

He hears a muffled, "Charles help me," from his left and sees a large stack of broken 2x4's stacked in a slant against the remaining wall of the barn.

"Charlotte," Charles frantically begins throwing the broken boards out of the way, revealing the old corncrib.

The hay inside the crib begins to move, then Charlottes head pokes through the straw.

"Charlotte, are you all right," Charles reaches out to her helping her out of the crib. He hugs her. She looks up to him with tears in her eyes as they stand holding each other.

Hebrew and Angela watch from a hilltop. They send Tote with the message to Michlu that Charles and Charlotte are ok.

* * *

Sam Donaldson slams the book closed, "Poppycock," he's been reading a book written by Herbert Winer about Darwinism.

"He still believes that malarkey," Sam storms from his coach throwing the book into a trash can.

Sam and Herbert have a life long rivalry about creationism, which dates back to their early college years at Missouri University at Columbia.

Sam was not a full time student, just taking a class on, "Relevant Religion in Today's Society," when he met Herbert and that is when the debates began.

Sam took offense when Herbert suggested that he quit going to, "...a fairy tale world of make believe," and place is mind back on the real truth of Darwinian Theory. After a brief argument Sam picked up Herbert throwing him into the schools fountain.

Since then, Sam's been a rebel against society's views on religion and how it is taught in schools. He spent 120 days in jail during the early 1960's, after he broke into his local high school and burned all the books teaching the, "Monkey Theory" as Sam calls it.

After prayer in schools was removed he protested by picketing the courthouse in Columbia, and throwing the local school administrator to the ground during an open debate in the Town Square. He spent three years in Fulton prison for that one.

Now, Sam is in his mid sixties with long gray hair, slim build, and muscular arms. He works for a local farmer in Lincoln County tending the fields, and working on machinery. He rents a small house, not far from his employer, where he writes to the Governor, and the President of the United States warning them of Armageddon, reads his Bible daily, and prays constantly.

He doesn't have to live here. Major newspapers across the country offered him jobs in the past to write columns about his research on Darwinian Theory. He is known world wide, but only as his pen name of, Walter Gulf. He fears that if he use's his real name it could expose his past. The world would see him as a radical and not as someone with creditability.

Sam opens an old wooden shed to get his gardening tools. When he's upset he works with his flowerbeds, this relaxes him. As he approaches the end of his drive he notices a Jeep parked next to his mailbox. A young woman standing near the jeep holds some kind of instrument up to her eyes looking through it.

"Hello," Sam yells while waving, still some distance from the Jeep.

The woman waves back then returns to her instrument. He arrives at the Jeep smiling at her, "Hi! My name is Sam, and who are you?"

"Hi, my name is Sharon," she doesn't know what to think of

this man in front of her with his shoulder length gray hair, and bib-overalls.

"You're English," Sam asks after hearing her Aussie voice.

"No, I'm from Sydney Australia," Sharon smiles.

"Wow, Sydney! What brings you and that device all the way to my driveway? It certainly isn't me, or my flowers," Sam chuckles and she smiles.

"Well, actually your flowers are wonderful, but that isn't why I'm here," She points to the horizon at dark gray storm clouds, "That's why I'm here, and this is a handheld Laser GPS Transit. It will tell me how far away those clouds are and how fast their moving."

"That is cool, so you're some kind of weatherman…weather person?"

Sharon laughs, "Yes, yes I'm a meteorologist. And I'm trying to get a reading on those clouds because they seem to be moving this way."

"Yes, those clouds are a welcome sight. We certainly need the rain." Sam looks at Sharon as she lowers her GPS.

"You don't know do you," Sharon looks at him quizzically.

"Know what?"

"The danger of these storms, what, do you live in a cave back there? These storms are causing a lot of flooding and washing away everything in Warren County, and now they're in western St. Charles County. You should be thankful you're not washed away and…"

Sam cuts her off, "Wait now. Slow down. Explain to me what's happening."

Sharon explains why she was sent, and whom she works for. Then she details the intensity of the storms, "…then I took some photos, and video of the wall," she stops short of telling Sam about the images, "I can't believe you haven't seen any of this on the news or heard it on the radio, Sam."

"Well, I have heard about the flooding in Warren County, and I have seen the wall on local news broadcast. The news reports say the cell is moving east, and losing intensity."

As Sam and Sharon stand by Sam's mailbox a long caravan of military vehicles roar past, "The reserves," Sam points to the vehicles as they pass, "…they've been going by here regularly for the last couple weeks. I think they have a camp set up down the road by Cuiver River."

"Yes, their helping to control the flooding in the low lands. The rain washes everything away, and then carries it off through creek beds to the Missouri, and the Mississippi River flood plains," Sharon puts the GPS down on top of the hood of her Jeep, and then turns facing Sam, "How long have you lived here, Sam?"

"Oh, I lived in Missouri most of my life, but only four years here."

"How well do you know this area?"

"Pretty good I guess, is there some place you need to go?"

Sharon walks around her Jeep to the passenger side and retrieves a topographical map of the area from the glove box. She spreads the map over the hood pointing to a spot on the map, "There! That's where I want to go, but I can't seem to find a way to it. All the roads are flooded, and helicopter pilots won't fly in the storm."

"Why would you want to go there? The rain started there last night and the areas closed by the National Guard."

"I need some firsthand steady from inside the wall, Sam."

"Why don't we get in out of this heat Sharon? I think it's affected your common sense," Sam gently pats Sharon on the back, "Now, come on and let's get a cool drink."

Sharon and Sam walk back to Sam's house. Sitting in the living room drinking lemonade Sharon notices several books lying on the coffee table, "You read this," Sharon asks while holding up one of Sam's books, authored by his alias, Walter Gulf.

"Why yes I do, marvelous writer, unparalleled in his field. Have you read any of his books," Sam brags.

"No, I was just wondering if you were doing some research or just have concerns about evolution," Sharon puts the book back on the table sipping her drink.

"It's a complicated story and I'm sure you don't have time to hear it all, but I will tell you this much, evolution is a theory, nothing more, and nothing less. God didn't make us out of an ape. He formed us with his hands, and blew life into us through our nostrils."

Michlu sits beside Sharon and whispers, "Sam is your friend. Take him with you."

"Sam, that's great. I'm glad you feel that way, because that is the way I feel also. Listen, I don't know why, but for some reason I feel you need to be involved in what I'm doing here."

Michlu continues to whisper.

"...and I'm not sure why, but I must explain something to you," Sharon says and takes a sip of lemonade.

Sharon explains to Sam about the images. She sets up her laptop showing Sam the images.

Michlu stands next her staring at the image, and listening to the voice. Hanna stands next to Sam, and whispers, "I know you feel she is crazy, and that she made this whole thing up, but she didn't. Listen to her, and help her," Michlu and Hanna then leave.

"Is that Jesus," Sharon points to the faded image on her screen.

"I don't think so. God wouldn't show himself this way, I don't think...err I mean, he can show himself anyway he wants, but you know, I really do not know," Sam feels confused and quickly changes the subject, "What is Nicboth and why would God be telling you to go there? Are you sure he is speaking to you," Sam asks gently.

"I don't know Sam. I sent this to my colleague, Bruce in Sydney, and he didn't see anything. My boss promised to look at it. Sam, I'm sure not going crazy. After all you see it, you hear it," Sharon says excited.

Sam pats her on the shoulder, "You're not crazy. Something extraordinary is happening here, and I understand why you feel you must go into the wall now," Sam walks across the room and opens a small closet door. He begins pulling out wet gear, and flashlights. "If we are going into that mess we'll need some protection. Here, take this out to your jeep."

Chapter 4
Transition of Power

Clouds roll across the Heavens on strong winds aloft. An earthly a breeze rattles an old weather vein atop Charles old barn, albeit leaning sideways on the collapsed roof.

"It's just not safe here Charlotte."

Charles tries to convince his wife to leave the washed out farm and seek help.

"Look honey, the barn is a shambles, and the house is ready to fall. The truck is flipped over, and if we don't find a way out of here soon the next storm is going to drown us," He lifts her hand to his lips and kisses the back of it. Looking at her, he sees a tear forming in the corner of her eye.

Her lips quiver, and her eyes squint pushing the tears out, they run down her cheeks. She understands it isn't she that Charles is trying to convince, but himself.

Charlotte wraps her arms lovingly around him, "If you think it's the best thing to do honey, then we must go," Charlotte speaks softly as she lowers her hands from around his back. She takes his hand, "Lets go."

On the horizon they see dark clouds swell.

Reaching the main asphalt road they sit down on its shoulder to rest. The weight of the mud on their shoes makes walking difficult. As Charles cleans Charlotte's shoes he looks up at her in time to see her fall limp over him. He holds her tenderly while he lays her on the asphalt watching her body lay still, motionless. Her breathing is steady, but labored. He holds her head up wiping the sweat from her forehead, "Charlotte, oh honey."

Hebrew points to the horizon at the storm clouds, and sends Angela to Charles. Hebrew then takes flight to the clouds. As he approaches the storm two large warriors from Bels army, Maglic and Draw, meet him.

"Where do you think your going Hebrew," Maglic demands as he pulls his sword.

Hebrew pulls his sword stopping within a sword length of them, "Out of my way Maglic, you have no govern over me."

"Oh, but we do Hebrew. This is our finest hour and you will be in submission to me," Maglic plunges his sword at Hebrew; Draw swings his staff at Hebrews head.

Hebrew is the master of weaponry wielding his sword with purposeful might. He blocks Maglic plunge, then chops Draw staff in two with one swipe of his sword. Draw retreats, as Maglic stands ready to attack.

"You won't win like you did at the garden," warns Maglic, "...there you had help. Now, it's just you and me," Maglic lunges twice at Hebrew, but misses.

"If you hadn't joined the others in rebellion, Maglic, you would be one of the Lords best," Hebrew blocks several more of Maglic thrusts, "I defend as the Lord commands. At the garden you caused the disciples to sleep. You also caused Peter to attack the Roman solider, cutting off his ear."

Hebrew thrust his sword forward knocking Maglic's sword

out of his hand. Then before Maglic has time to react he presses the point of his sword against Maglic throat, "With the help of the Lord I stopped you then and now," Hebrew glares into Maglic's eyes. He wants to push harder taking Maglic's life, but that is not Gods desire. Hebrew lowers his sword, stepping back from Maglic, "Go, tell Bel his time is short."

Maglic scowls at Hebrew while rubbing his hairy throat, "Don't think so highly of your God. We are mightier than you think," Maglic takes flight.

Hebrew continues toward the storm as dark clouds bellow around him. Ahead of him he sees a thousand demons standing guard next to the gate of Ramtu. This gate is the entrance to the clouds strength, where Hebrew needs to go to stop the storm. Maglic once again confronts him with the demons hovering behind him. Hebrew dives low into the clouds before retreating back to Angela. He will face Maglic another day.

Maglic considers pursuing him, "We'll let the storm take care of his charges," Maglic laughs.

Angela is standing near Charles watching the storms advance. Hebrew lands next to them, "Will she be ok," he asks standing over Charlotte.

"Yes, but we need to get them into safety," Angela takes flight to look for shelter.

Hebrew whispers to Charles, "She'll be ok. You must find shelter," Charles sits on the ground, with Charlotte lying on his lap. Her head lies on Charles left arm, while he holds her hands praying for the first time in many years he remembers the mounds.

"Your prayers are heard Charles," Hebrew whispers. Charles suddenly looks up the road when he hears the sound of a vehicle approaching. He waves his arm and yells, "Help, you must stop… Help!"

"Look," Sam points to a man beside the road holding a woman in his arms.

"Looks like they could use our help," Sharon stops the Jeep next to them. Sam and Sharon rush to Charles side.

"Is she hurt," Sam asks.

"She, she is sick," Charles stammers, "We have to get her to a hospital."

"Ok, sure, let's get her into the Jeep. The nearest hospital is in Wentzville, and that's some miles away," As Sam speaks he can see the storm coming over the hill, "Hurry, let's move!"

Sharon and Sam lift Charlotte into the back seat of the Jeep then help Charles in next to her, "Where to Sam, and I mean some place close," Sharon urgently asks.

"We don't have much choice right now. Go forward until you see a sign with a cow on it, on your right." Charles instructs, "…then turn right."

Sharon cuts him off, "But that will put us directly in the storms path."

"It's ok…There is an old military armory 50 yards or so in the woods. Completely abandon and unlocked. Kids use it for parties and things," Charles assures Sharon.

"There's the sign Sharon, turn here," Sam points to a small white sign with a picture of a cow on it. Sharon turns the Jeep right onto an old rock-clay road.

"There by that fallen tree, turn left there," Charles points to a large log, and Sharon turns down a muddy wagon path. She can see five large mounds of dirt lined up in a row,

"You mean those mounds," Sharon questions.

"Yes, those are the storage areas used during World War II. The military made bombs at Weldon Springs and had many areas in St. Charles County where they stored things. This is one of them. Go to the last one up there," Charles explains.

Sharon stops the Jeep next to the last mound. On the far side of the mound is a rusty riveted metal door already open. Sam and Charles carry Charlotte in while Sharon uses some blankets from the Jeep to place on the concrete floor for Charlotte to lie on. Sam tries to close the door, but it won't stay shut. Beer cans, paper, old magazines, and other trash litter the floor. Graffiti covers the walls, with the stench of mildew filling their nostrils. Charles sits besides Charlotte holding her in his arms. Sam and Sharon stand at the entrance watching the storm move closer. Sharon has her camera and video camera with her. Sam is also looking at Sharon's map.

"Sharon, isn't this the spot you pointed to on the map," Sam points to a spot with a blue dot on it.

"Yes, it is. Hey! Wait a minute. If I'm seeing this correctly we are right here, right now," Sharon stares in amazement.

"How could that be," Sam wonders.

"You're here because God wants you here," Hebrew says boldly.

"Did you hear that," Sharon asks.

"It was angels," Charles shouts above the storm, "Charlotte told me to tell you."

Sharon and Sam stare at Charles in disbelief. The wind suddenly bangs the door against its frame. The wind howls past the old door squeaking on its rusty hinges.

"Well, whatever it was, I think we should pay attention. I'm going outside to get a shot," Sharon says while looking around then steps out of the mound. She stands outside the door with her video-camera ready to film.

Sam walks over to the door propping a large rock in front of it to hold it open.

The wind bangs the door against the rock, as large drops of rain pour from the sky. Lighting strikes, while thunder echoes around them. Sam grabs Sharon's arm pulling her into the mound.

Sharon regains her footing, "Thanks," she yells at Sam, "I missed my shot!"

"I'm sorry, Sharon, but you shouldn't be outside," Sam apologies shrugging his shoulders.

Sharon glares at Sam then steps toward the door just as the wall strikes. Rain pours in front of her rushing away from the sloping mound. She begins filming the water pouring outside of the door. Through the viewfinder she sees the image of a man standing in the doorway, "Sam, do…do you see anything in the doorway," Sharon stammers.

"No, just the rain. Why," Sam asks while looking at Sharon who holds the camera shaking.

"Come, come over here, and look," Sharon says nervously.

Sam steps over to Sharon then looks through the viewfinder. To Sam's surprise he sees a man dressed as a roman solider staring straight at him, "Yes, yes I see him. He's saying something," Sam hands the camera back to Sharon.

"What in the world are you two talking about? There isn't anyone at that door," Charles yells over the thundering torrent.

"He's saying, 'three, look in three,'" Charlotte struggles to speak.

Charles leans his ear closer to Charlottes, "Charlotte, how do you feel sweetie," Charles kisses her on the forehead. Sam kneels near her holding her hand. Sharon looks through the viewfinder again, and the image is gone.

Charlotte looks into Charles eyes, "He wants them to look into the third bunker Charles. Didn't any of you hear him," Sam pats Charlotte's hand.

"You heard him? She heard him Sam…how," Sharon and Sam look at each other baffled.

The Rain suddenly stops.

"Go now, look in the third bunker," Charlotte waves her hand and motions them out the door.

Sam and Sharon look at each other then walk out the door still in awe at what happened.

Dark gray clouds roll above them, as the wind stirs the limbs of trees. A fine mist fills the air. Sam struggles to see through the mist.

"Well, I guess were in number five," Sam points to the number above the doorway chiseled into the concrete, "And I guess that's number three," Sam motions to a bunker two mounds away.

The condition of number three is the same as number five. Sam and Sharon kick around the trash, but find nothing. A wind slowly begins swirling the trash around before fading. Sam sees a rusty two-by-two lid built into the concrete floor in the center of the mound.

"Look," Sam points to the rusty lid, "What is this?"

Sam uses his pocketknife to loosen the lid. He preys the heavy lid up with a piece of scrap metal, sliding it to the side revealing a deep dark vault.

Sharon rushes back to her Jeep, sloshing through the mud to retrieve a flashlight, then hurries back to Sam. Sam shines the light into the deep void onto an old metal chest covered with dust. He brushes away the dust to reveal the words, "Top Secret" stenciled on its top.

Sam looks at Sharon, "Oh may, what do we have here?"

The chest is heavy, but Sam has no problem pulling the chest out of the vault. An old lock holds the chest's lid tight. Sharon finds an old pipe cracking the lock open after several hard hits.

"Well, go ahead and open it," Sharon says excitedly.

Slowly—Sam opens the lid.

"We have to do something," snarls Dart who has watched over the chest for 56 years, but Hebrew stands in his way.

"We, oh no you have it all wrong. We don't have to do anything. You do! I came here to keep you company. You will have to answer to Maglic," Leper laughs pointing at Hebrew, "You let him just walk right in here and didn't try to stop him. It would be better if Hebrew cuts you with his sword, rather than have nothing to show for your efforts over all these years," Leper laughs.

"Ok, I'll stop them," Dart draws his sword leaping at Hebrew swinging his sword wildly from side to side.

Hebrew draws his sword, swinging it effortlessly striking Dart's sword snapping it in two. Dart lands on his side sliding across the bunker.

"Ok, I tried! I'm out of here," Dart hastily takes flight, while Leper continues to laugh uncontrollably. Hebrew walks over to Leper placing the point of his sword under Lepers chin.

"I think it's time for you to leave and join your little friend," Hebrew smiles at Leper.

Leper tries to stop laughing, "Ok…Ooo…k, I'm going. Oh that was too much, too much," Leper finally controls himself taking flight after Dart, "Hey wait up!"

Sam and Sharon leaf through manila envelopes full of classified military documents from WWII.

"We have to get this out of here and take it someplace safe," Sharon says while closing the chest. Sam nods in agreement. They carry the chest back to Bunker 5.

"How are you feeling Charlotte," Sharon asks while kneeling beside her.

Charlotte nods her head, "I see you found something, good. I knew you would. Then she coughs.

"We need to get her out of here and to a hospital. Do you think it's safe now," Charles asks while rubbing Charlotte's hands.

"Yes, the storm has moved off, and the sun is peeking through. Let's go," Sharon helps Charlotte to her feet. Sam and Charles pick up the cameras and each carries an end of the chest.

"What's this," Charles asks while lifting the chest.

"I'm not sure. It's full of old documents, and photos from World War Two. I think this is why Sharon was directed here and…" Sam stops himself. He isn't sure how much to tell Charles.

"Directed," Charles smiles at Sam, "…sounds like you need to tell me more young man."

Sharon lowers the small tailgate of the Jeep. Sam and Charles slid the heavy box under the back seat of the jeep then close the gate.

* * *

Bel sits on a rock looking out over the Pacific. The solitude helps him regain focus and composure. The soft roar of the surf washes up on the beach mixes with the calmness of the night soothing his senses, renewing his thoughts. He looks up into the Heavens at the stars at their magnificent beauty. Thoughts drift to a more pleasant time when life didn't consist of war and bloodshed. Those countless lights filling the sky in twinkling clusters reminds him of journeys he took when his life was different—peaceful.

Over time he had almost forgotten the path he choose placing him where he is now; the leader of a large band of rebel angles, the slave to Que, and the enemy of God. Sometimes he wonders if he made the right choice during the rebellion. He lays back on the rock folding his arms behind his head. Still looking up at the stars his eyes suddenly grow heavy, he falls into a deep sleep.

Guards posted all around Bel at a distance during these times of solitude keep their post stand on the ready. One guard, however, likes to look around. He too likes to look at the Heavens, gaze at the stars. He turns toward Bel, seeing him asleep wonders if Bel is dead, possibly struck by some unseen force. Angels and demons do not sleep.

He moves closer to Bel, "Commander," he whispers, "Commander, are you alright," The guard steps cautiously closer. Using the, butt of his spear he gently pokes Bel's leg, "Commander," Bel opens his eyes, sitting up suddenly, gasping.

"What happened? What...oh," Bel groggily looks around, confused by his sleep and the dream he had, "What are you doing here," Bel snaps at the guard, "Get back to your post!"

The guard moves back to his position. Bel sits still on the rock rubbing his forehead.

"I can't believe this...this can't be happening to me. Not me," his thoughts are riddled with fragmented memories. For the first time in many years he almost mumbles a prayer to God, "What, No! What am I doing? I have to get a grip."

Bel looks out across the ocean. The evening fog settles on the horizon moving toward shore.

"Guards, pull back into camp. Jorge, bring Python to my tent," Bel shouts orders as the guards gather around him preparing for the short march back to camp.

The fog quickly engulfs the island, smothering the trail in a thick dense blanket of white.

"Halt," Bel shouts.

Even though the guards and Bel can hear each other, they can only see faint images of one another.

"Jorge, go ahead. Make sure the path is clear. Frit fly overhead, find a way around this mess. The rest of you listen...keep your senses open," Bel doesn't like this.

He knows Jobauten will try to take advantage of the fog. They must find a way back to the safety. A few minutes pass then ahead of him Bel sees a shadow moving toward him.

He silently draws his sword.

"Jorge," he stretches his senses to feel who this shadow might be, but his senses are numb.

"Frit, Nombe, Debar," Bel shouts for his guards, but no response.

The shadow steps closer.

"Halt! I command you to halt," Bel shouts at the advancing figure.

The full moon light filtered by the dense cloud creates a grayish hue all around. Bel stands ready to fight this ghostly shadow approaching him. He lifts his sword ready to strike, when the figure illuminates with an intense blinding white light. The fog moves away from the shadowy figure and Bel creating a dome over them.

Bel lowers his hand to see an image of an angle clothed in pure white from shoulder to ankle with wings folded on its back. Bel now recognizes who it is. Dropping his sword he falls to his knees, the angel is Ethane.

Ethane trained Bel in Heaven guiding him through out the stars; educating him; teaching him the ways of God and finally rejected him after the rebellion. Bel has no power against him.

"What do you want with me Lord," Bel asks.

Ethane reaches down lifting Bel to his feet, "I'm not your Lord, Bel. Stand and talk with me."

As Bel stands he feels his strength return, his fear leaves. He feels a quiet sense all around him. A different time returns to his mind. A time when Ethane and he were best of friends, a time when the only purpose for being was doing Gods will.

"I'm here to reveal to you the dream you had," Ethane, says smiling.

"Dream...yes, I did see things when my eyes were closed," Bel slowly speaks.

"Sleeping is new to you, as it should be. Man sleeps, and animals sleep, but angels do not...not even the fallen ones," Ethane paces in small steps while talking, "The dream you had was a message from God to you. You saw a wall of rain pouring out of Heaven onto to dry ground. The waters gathered into a great lake, and those that drank from the water were suddenly transformed, and lifted up into Heaven. Those that refused to drink withered and were scorched by an extreme heat until the wind blew their dust away."

Ethane stops his pacing in front of Bel pointing at him. His voice becomes deep, and harsh, "You listen to this interpretation Bel; you were created by God for his purpose and no other," Bel drops to his knees, covering his ears, "...you threw that all away to follow Lucifer into the burning pit. Gods' son will be returning very soon. The day and the hour God only knows. Before this happens he offers you redemption—he extends his pierced hands to you! The Lord wants you to drink from his lake of goodness, and not be blown away by the wind of unrighteousness," Ethane's eyes look deep into Bels eyes then he gently helps Bel to his feet again, "Pray Bel...seek him again," Ethane smiles then disappears.

The light fades casting a deep darkness around Bel. The dome collapses allowing the dense grayish cloud to once again surround him.

Before Bel can gather his thoughts Jorge shouts, "Commander, the path is clear."

Frit shouts, "Commander, there isn't anyway around this, but the fog is lifting."

Bel commands them to wait for the fog to lift. The guards sit mulling over a defense if Jobauten should attack, but Bel sits thinking about Ethane.

The fog lifts and the path is clear. They march down a twisting path lined by dense foliage, and with patches of open fields of tall grass. Bels mind is not on Jobauten, or his encampment, but on the dream, while inside his soul wrestles in twisted confusion.

As they reach their camp, Python flutters down from a tall palm, "Bel, we've been waiting for your return. Jobauten wants a counsel with you," Python motions to Jobauten who is sitting on a stump across the camp.

Python then flies over to Jobauten hovering carelessly above him, "Bel is here and will see you now and," Before Python can finish his sentence, Jobauten swats him out of the sky with his open palm sending the little demon tumbling through the air into a bush near by.

Bel draws his sword.

"Jobauten, are you here to fight or talk," Bel shouts grabbing Jobauten by the collar of his garment lifting him off the ground—holding him at arms length. Bel places the point of his sword in Jobauten's stomach, "We can end this now, or later it is your choice," Bel sneers.

Jobauten struggles to turn his head looking down at Bel, then grins devilishly at him, "You're really ambitious for one who dreams."

Bel loosens his grip dropping Jobauten to the ground. Bel stands over him, sheathing his sword while looking intently at Jobauten.

"What do you know, and how do you know it," Bel stands leering down at Jobauten.

Jobauten stands smiling again.

"Oh, that little dream you had while you were, 'composing yourself.' That would be an interesting thing for Que to find out,"

Jobauten paces in front of Bel, "Now, I don't know what the dream was about, but Que will. How do you suppose he will like it Bel?"

"Enough of this... Yes, I did dream," Bel walks over to Jobauten with a lighting fist knocking Jobauten to the ground. All the hate inside him comes pouring forth as he strikes Jobauten over and over again while shouting, "Que knows all! My loyalty is to him, and no other!"

Bel leers down at Jobauten who is trying to crawl away.

Jobauten is weak from the punishing blows. He pushes himself up with his arms, but is unable to rise any further. Bel draws his sword. He raises the razor sharp blade above his head then sends it plunging deep into Jobautens chest. Green smoke rushes out of the wound swirling around them.

"To the burning pit you—vermin," Bel shouts. He staggers backward dropping his sword, lowers his head in prayer to Que, then falls to his knees.

Jobauten presses both hands on the gaping wound trying to hold in the green essence. Smoke trickles through his fingers and out of the corners of his mouth swirling around his head.

"The," Jobauten struggles to speak as the green smoke grows thicker around them, "...the dream....I lied..."

Bel lifts his head turning to Jobauten.

Jobauten stares into Bel's eyes, "...I lied—I know...what your dream was about..." Jobauten coughs and spits, his voice becomes rasp, congested by the smoke now flowing freely from his nose and mouth, "...all demons desire to gain what they have lost. You..." He swallows and coughs, "...you have a chance, a chance to get back what you gave up...do...not...pass it up."

Jobauten then rolls onto his back. The green smoke thickens surrounding the lifeless demon. His body degenerates, crumbling into a pile of dust that the wind carries away along with the smoke.

The wind lifts Jobautens remains high in the sky where his guards watch his essence float past.

Above Bels head he hears the chattering of a thousand demons, along with the deafening flutter of their wings. The full moon disappears, blotted out by their numbers.

"To arms! Stations," Bel shouts commands as his army mobilizes.

Python, still reeling from his encounter with Jobauten watches as the last of Jobauten's remains blow away; he smiles then joins the others. Bels troops quickly gather in battle formation as the now leaderless army of Jobautens dives recklessly upon them. Trumpeters signal the attack, and like locust the demons descend from the night sky beginning their assault.

Load shouts, screams, and vulgar obscenities utter from this dark cloud of anger. The sounds of battle rage on all corners of the darkened island, demon against demon.

Swords clang against sword and as demons fall puffs of green smoke bellow then drift on the wind into the distant horizon.

Que stands on a cloud in the distance listening. The green smoke swirls around him and he inhales deeply drawing the smoke into his nostrils. The sounds excite him luring him to become part of the battle. This is his plan though. He is tired of division in his ranks. Only the strong will survive, only one leader will emerge.

Bel leaps onto a large rock warding off an attack by two-pint size demons. They hop on their back legs then spring forward. One plunges a sword while the other shoots arrows. Bel dives off the rock, rolls to his feet while swinging his sword upward cutting one lizard in two. The other continues to pursue him with the arrows.

"So, you're Bel! Your the one who failed at the cross roads! Die you scum," the little demon cackles.

The demon shoots four arrows in succession. Bel dodges two, while deflecting the others with his sword. With a spin he swats the demon with his sword, smashing him like a fly. Small green puffs of smoke roll out from under the sword.

All around him he can hear the battle in full fury. Through the night the battle rages. By morning few find the courage to continue.

Bel stands on the beach with two hundred of his demons with their backs to the sea. He retreated to the beach alone while being pursued by four demons. While he fought, one of his demons appeared from the jungle, forced back by several smaller ones. Then another and another, all herded to this spot.

A gauntlet of angry demons approaches their front. Yesterday, Bel outnumbered those, three to one, now the numbers reversed. Bel is desperate to turn the odds to his favor.

The band of demons stops their assault. Heath, Jobautens second in command walks out to meet Bel.

Bel knows this one from Eden.

"Surrender Bel, it is over. Look at you. You stand ready to fight and there's no use." Heath laughs, "We'll just cut you to shreds like we did the rest."

Bel never surrenders unless command to, and he hasn't received those orders. Gritting his teeth he glares at Heath. He stands a few yards in front of Heath swinging his sword from side to side ready to pounce. His army is ready to attack.

"We have you surrounded, and outnumbered. Put down your weapons and surrender your command to me," Heath demands.

Bels hears the words, but is focused on another voice whispering…into his soul.

"Attack," Bel yells the command as he plunges his sword deep into Heaths chest. His remnants immediately follow attacking the shocked demons.

The two armies clash as Bels forces begin pushing the demons back into the jungle. One by one Jobautens mighty army falls. Bels forces fight with a renewed strength wielding their swords in precise motions. A new power engulfs them.

In the mourning sky an aerial battle begins. Demons from both sides dive in and out of clouds throwing spears, shooting arrows, some wrestle in hand to hand combat. Python wrestles one onto the beach stabbing the demon through the chest. He takes flight to pursue another, but they are none left.

The once mighty army of Bels is gone, reduced to one hundred. They land on the beach exhausted.

Bel sits down under a tree, and removes his helmet. He is glad it is finished, but when he thinks of the cost he is overwhelmed and kneels to pray to Que for guidance.

Python flutters down landing near him. He quietly sits.

"What now, Bel? Should we celebrate, or ask Que for re-enforcements," Python smirks.

"You know what to do," Bel smiles at him as he leans back on the tree.

"You're the only commander left. No one else is here. From the beginning you were with Que. Now, you're second only to Que," Python gets down on his knees and begins bowing, "All hale the great Bel, the commander of Que's army. Hale, Hale…"

Bel slowly turns his head looking at Python who is looking at Bel, chuckling. Bel then begins to laugh.

On a cloud opposite of Que two angels watch the battle.
"We've lost him again," Ethane says with a tear in his eye.
"We never had him," Michlu answers.

***

"Senator," shouts a reporter trying to get Newton's attention, "What does the government plan to do about the Midwest?"

Newton is in a hurry.

He is late; the reporter is a waste of time.

The rain pours down in Washington D.C. as the cold December air chills him. The Senate is in full session today, most waiting in anticipation of his speech on the threat of Global Warming then a vote before their break begins. Newton rushes toward the chambers.

The reporter has followed him all the way from his car onto the steps leading into the private entrance of the Senate hall.

"Senator! Please, does the government even care about their citizens?"

Newton abruptly stops.

He turns and faces the reporter glaring at him, "I know the Midwesterners are in need of federal aid, and yes, we are concerned about our citizens. If you want answers to your questions you should be asking the President. Not I," Newton turns, marching toward the door.

The reporter continues yelling question following Newton up the stairs where several guards step in grabbing the reporter by the arms.

Newton reaches the door sliding his pass-card through the lock. The door clicks several times, then he punches several numbers into a special panel on the side of the door. The door clicks several more times, followed by a beep indicating he is free to enter. After entering, and going through several more check points, Newton finds himself on the Senate floor. He checks over his speech, then feels a sudden clam come over him. To everyone he appears normal; he exchanges pleasantries, dabbles in small talk, but on the inside he knows something is wonderfully different. He feels very confident about his speech. Never in all his days on the Senate floor has he ever felt so relaxed.

After his introduction he takes his position behind the podium. In the front row are the Lawyers. He looks out at the entire chamber filled with Senators, lobbyist, and guest.

He smiles, and begins, "Ladies and Gentleman of the Senate. I stand here before you today after completing a five-year study on Global Warming. My staff and I, over these five years, employed some of the best meteorological scientist in the world to study, and write about this issue. We've gathered evidence from over a thousand studies on this topic which lay in front of you today. The conclusion of all this is the world is warming at a rate faster than anyone ever thought. Senators, at the rate we are warming, the polar icecaps will be melted by this time three years from now. This means the flooding in the Midwest will be nothing in comparison. The sea level will raise eighty feet worldwide. Some speculate even one hundred. I must admit, like many of you I was skeptical of this report, and did some investigative research myself and explored every realm of possibilities to assure the accuracy. I found no fault. The facts presented to you are true and clear based on findings from some of foremost experts in this field. Now, here is my challenge to you. Take the information I've given you, and do your own study. You will find all this to be true, but, after you finish your study, the situation will be worse. Time is running out. We have citizens in harms way that we must save without alarming them. We have a world that sits unaware of this report, and its findings. We must warn them so they to can take precautions against the raising seas."

Newton's face becomes enraged, and he slams his fist hard against the podium, then he points his finger at the Senate, as his eyebrows narrow, and point inward. His teeth clench together, and his lips draw thin. His rigid finger points across the room, as he waves it at the audience.

"It will be all of you that the country and the world will blame if these things I foretold to you come to pass and you do nothing to help save them."

He pauses, and listens to the silence in the room.

The Senators eyes and ears directed toward him in complete submission to his powerful tantrums.

"Read the report, and then let's vote to send this to the Congress for approval. Meanwhile listen to what this bill proposes,

First, a new land mass will emerge from the melting ice caps. As stated the Mississippi, Ohio, and Missouri valleys will be covered in water. Florida will be a thin strip of land while most of our cost lines will also, be submerged. The great lakes will swell and flood the surrounding areas. We must make ready our levies and dams to contain this massive amount of water.

Second, we must seek the aid of our neighbors lending then workers, if needed, to help in this time of climatic atmospheric anomalies. This is not an impossible task if we start now, but will become one of desperation if we wait."

A Senator stands in the back of the room and shouts, "Lets vote now," another stands, "Now is the time, lets vote."

A murmur of approval begins soft, and then all in the audience loudly agree to vote on Newton's bill.

"Thank you! Thank you all for the overwhelming support, but you first, must read the report, and then we'll vote. I do not want any doubters."

Newton steps down from the podium, and begins to walk away, when a spattering of applauds starts, followed by a roar of applauds from the audience of Senators. He stops and turns to find them standing, applauding loudly. He smiles.

Ce directs his squad to stay with each member of the Senate making sure they read the bill.

"What do we do now," questions Silt.

"We wait for Bel to command us. We will make sure the Senators do not find fault with the bill," answers Ce.

* * *

Bruce stands by the printer retrieving a print out of the latest data about the storm. He tears the form from the machine. For a moment he studies the numbers, then returns to his desk where he begins punching numbers into his calculator.

"Ben, I think you need to see this," Bruce doesn't take his eyes off the paper, "Ben," Bruce speaks a little louder. He then peeks over his paper to find Ben staring at the Laptop on his desk, "Ben, are you all right," Bruce asks as he walks over to Ben's desk.

Ben sits very still, non-respondent.

"Ben," Bruce tries to get Ben's attention by waving the paper around in the air, "Oh Ben...earth to Ben...captain, I think we have a communications problem...Scotty, more speed...Ben," Bruce continues until he reaches Ben's desk.

Bruce looks over Bens shoulder at the screen. He sees the picture of the right fender of Sharon's Jeep, and the wall, "Isn't that amazing, a wall of rain pouring straight down out of the sky," Bruce leans closer to the PC monitor lowering his head within several inches of Ben's.

"You don't know how close you are to the truth of the matter young man," Ben softly speaks, "Do you see anything else besides rain, Bruce?"

"No, nothing, but a wall of water. You know, Sharon asked me the same question," Bruce stands up looking puzzled at Ben, "What do you see?"

"Bruce, do you believe in God? Not only God, but his son," Ben turns in his chair facing Bruce.

"Well, I believe in God. The creator of all things, but that Christmas story isn't real," Bruce is still looking at the picture, "Hey, what did Sharon see Ben, do you see it too," Bruce asks as he looks closely at the picture on the monitor.

"There is a world that you don't know about, and things that I'm about to tell you, which you will not understand, unless I'm able to convince you that Christ is real," Ben says as he stands, then carefully steps by Bruce who is still looking closely at the picture. Ben walks across the room pulling a Bible off the bookshelf, "Do you really want to know what we see," Ben taps Bruce on the shoulder, and excuses himself as he steps again around Bruce to his chair.

"Yes, yes I would very much," Bruce quickly gets a chair and pulls it next to Ben's.

"Do you know what this is," Ben holds the Bible up and presents it Bruce, "It is the divine word of God. Not a book of religious mumbo jumbo, but rather the inspired word as written by those God has chosen to write it," Ben hands the book to Bruce.

"Ok, I know that is the common belief, and even if what you say is true how can it be authentic? After all, look at all the interpretations, and not only that, look at all the other religions that claim their, 'Bible' is also written and ordained by their God," Bruce puts out his hands and refuses to accept the book.

"Do you want to know what we see," Ben smiles at Bruce and pushes the Bible a little closer.

"Ok, yeah sure I do," Bruce takes the Bible from Ben's hand, and opens it, "Just what do you want me to look at anyway? Is what you see in here or on that monitor?"

"Both," Ben turns to the monitor, then begins to pray softly. He turns back to Bruce, "Have I ever told you how I got my limp?"

"No, I never asked, because I heard you got really mad if anyone asked," Bruce wiggles in his chair like a school kid waiting to be reprimanded.

"Well, that is true, but I'm ready to tell you if you promise not to tell anyone. It isn't often I open up like this."

Ben stands and walks over to the bookshelf again, retrieving a world atlas. He thumbs through it to a map of Africa.

"See that, that is the Congo in darkest Africa," Ben taps on the atlas handing it to Bruce, "I was eighteen, fresh out of high school. I joined my local church on a pilgrimage there. We brought blankets, food, and all sorts of medicines. It was going to be a wonderful adventure for me. I was so excited that I didn't sleep the whole night before we left. We arrived during the rainy season, and the rivers had flooded the roads. We had to take long detours to get across the few remaining bridges leading into the Congo. As we entered into the dense jungle the rain began to pour in torrents, much the same way as in Sharon's picture. We could actually see the wall of water as it came toward us in the few open patches beneath the jungle canopy. I was amazed at the intense down pours, and the brilliance of the lightning. It was there, huddled under large fumes that I saw him walking in the downpour. He motioned me to walk with him…"

"Wow, now wait a minute. Who is, 'he,' and this is beginning to sound like some wired attempt to get me to believe in your Christ," Bruce sits leaning forward in the chair, elbows on his knees, and his head upright.

"Do you want to know what we see," Ben points to the monitor.

"Sure, but…"

Ben cuts him off, "Good," Ben smiles at Bruce, "The person I saw in the Congo was Norwick…an Angle."

Bruce stands and walks toward his desk and then back to Ben's desk, "An angel! What do you mean an angel? You mean an angel, with wings and harps, and dressed in white," Bruce stammers.

Ben smiles, "Yes, and no. Now sit down here and let me explain."

Bruce hesitates.

"I assure you I've had my shots, and I don't bite very hard," Ben teases.

Bruce continues to stare wearily at Ben, as he cautiously sits down.

"Good! Now, like I said the shadowy image that beckoned is named Norwick. He is a fallen angel."

"Oh, like one of Lucifer's helpers, a demon? Yeah right," Bruce flops back in his chair and looks at the ceiling shaking his head, "…you really expect me to believe this?"

"My dear boy," Ben turns his chair toward Bruce's, and leans forward while placing his hands on Bruce's shoulders, "…there are angels sent by God to help us. There is the Holy Sprit that dwells inside all those that have chosen to follow Christ, and there are demons, fallen angels. Yes, you are right they are the devils helpers," Ben leans back in his chair and rest his elbows on the arm rest, while pointing a finger toward the floor, "…and they follow Lucifer even to hell."

"Wait, you mean these angels, these demons follow him to hell. Don't they know what hell is supposed to be," Bruce sits up in his chair, "Sounds like their devoted or just plain out of touch."

"Both," Ben smiles.

"I wish you would stop that Ben. I ask you a question and you tell me that both my guesses are right. You're confusing me," Bruce sets up straight in his chair waiting for Ben's response.

"Ok, maybe I should just continue with my story, and hopefully it will shed some light for you. Let's see...I was sitting under the flumes of a very large plant as the rain pounded all around me. It was raining so hard that I had to hold the flumes up to support them. As I looked into the dense downpour I saw someone moving a few feet in front of me. I couldn't see him clearly, just enough to tell he had a beard, and he was wearing some kind of outfit that reminded me of a Roman solider. He walked around in the rain, soak and wet, like there was no rain at all. Then, he looked at me straight into my eyes. I could feel warmth all over me as soon as our eyes made contact."

Ben covers his eyes, and rubs his forehead.

Bruce now sits in complete attention.

Ben lowers his hand and begins again, "He motioned for me to come out from under the flume, and come to him. I didn't want to at first, and was very hesitant to give up my, albeit, wet sanctuary, but he beckoned me on. I felt like I was in a dream. As I left the flumes and ventured into the pouring rain I noticed he was smiling. He began walking away, and then he motioned for me to follow. We entered into a small clearing with a thick canopy of limbs above it. The canopy acted as an umbrella keeping this area dry. He stopped and sat down next to a large tree trunk, and motioned for me to do the same. As I started to sit, I noticed something else. He didn't have a sword."

"Well...that's unusual, a gladiator without a sword," Bruce smiles at Ben.

"Ok, I know if I were hearing this I would be thinking this guy is a nut case too, but you haven't heard the good stuff yet."

Bruce leans back into his chair as Ben continues, "You see he didn't have a sword because it was taken from him by a demon general called Bel. You see Bruce; this isn't just any fallen angel, but one that rebelled against Que!"

"Que, you mean the devil."

"Yes and no…"

"There you go again," Bruce shouts.

"Listen; as we sat under the foliage I studied him. He sat on the ground, crossed leg, with the palms of his hands on his knees, and his head upright with his eyes closed. He didn't make a sound. This went on for some time, so I studied his appearance. All his facial features looked Roman; strong chin, sharp nose, high cheekbones, short Roman cut hair. His uniform reminded me of a Roman gladiator. He wore a bronze looking chest plate with another plate attached on the back. Under it he wore a red garment cut short at the sleeve. A thick leather belt held up his swag made of thick strips of leather with a red materiel sown in between each strip. His sandals were also made of leather with thick soles. The straps for the sandals warpped around his calf tightly. Attached to his belt hung an empty sheath for his sword. I wondered about his sword, and where it might be for the longest time. When he suddenly opened his eyes and spoke. He told me his name, Norwick, and that he was imprisoned by Bel for rebelling against the highest commander of them all, Que."

"Que is for all likelihoods the devil himself. You see the devil has armies, many vast armies, all around the world, and since he is not omnipresent like God, he needs these demon armies to be his eyes, ears, and sometimes his voice. Que is the devils highest commander, and Bel is Que's highest general," Ben stops for a moment and sips some coffee.

Bruce is staring at Ben, "Is any of this in the Bibl," Bruce asks while holding up the book.

"No, none of this is in the scriptures," Ben sits his coffee down, "…but you will find accounts of demons fighting angels, and being cast out of people."

"Then how can I believe any of what you're telling me Ben," Bruce lays the Bible down upon his lap.

"You'll see Bruce," Ben continues, "...well then, Norwick was Bel's right hand. He was right there at Heavens gate when Lucifer first talked rebelliously against God. Norwick was so convinced that Lucifer should replace God that when the rebellion broke out and swords were drawn he fought through six hundred angels, clearing a path for Lucifer to escape. He continued the fight as God sweep them out of Heaven and onto Earth. He was there in Eden and watched as Adam fell out of grace. He was there with David and tempted him all throughout his reign. Many men fell to his power of persuasion. After Jesus arrived Norwick found the truth. He saw the birth, the life, the death, the resurrection, and the accession of Jesus."

"He was in the meeting rooms helping to plot plans to deceive the Jews and to destroy the Son of man when he was overwhelmed by the mockery of his crime. He told everyone that they were wrong, and that they would never defeat God. He warned them Lucifer was leading them all into destruction and that Lucifer knew he couldn't win. Thousands of demons attacked him at once, and somehow he defeated them all. He knelt and prayed to God for forgiveness, and began the journey back to Heaven's gate when Bel confronted him. After a fierce struggle Norwick was defeated by Bel, and Que cast him into Gerdedabud, a place of constant rain." Ben stops and takes a drink of coffee.

He continues, "The rain is like bars to Norwick now that Que has rebuked Norwick's strength. He is trapped in this prison forever. After he finished explaining this to me the rain subsided and he was gone," Ben sets back in his chair.

"Is that it," Bruce asks wide-eyed.

"No, oh no," Ben continues, "I felt something strange inside of me, and I began reading the Bible a lot more. During this same time in the Congo, we met different native tribes. One tribe in particular took a special interest in me, and kidnapped me during the night staking me with the intent of burning me alive. The witchdoctor from the tribe came over to me, spit in my face, then whispered in my year, 'Norwick is watching this. Bel is laughing, Jesus is nothing, and Que will win the world for Lucifer.' Then he took a large poll and smacked my thigh repeatedly. Just as he was ready to start the fire a large wind came. Bringing with it lots of rain. Just as suddenly as it started it was over. The ropes binding me to the stake were gone along with the witchdoctor and tribesmen. I hobbled back to camp and the next day we started the journey home. The whole trip home only took a few days, but it seemed like years. My hip felt like it was on fire, and when the doctors on the ship looked at it they found what they said were splinters of shattered bone. After I arrived in Sydney, our family doctors had my hip x-rayed. They confirmed the ship doctors fears…the ball of the hip was splintered. They operated replacing the ball with an artificial ball joint. That is why I limp," Ben pauses pointing to the monitor, "Norwick is who Sharon and I see in the picture, but I do not think he is calling Sharon to Nicboth, but me."

Ben swings his chair around toward his desk and stairs at the picture on the monitor. He is not expecting Bruce to believe his story, and isn't really sure what to say if he doesn't.

Bruce leans back in his chair with his right elbow on the armrest. He is rubbing his chin with his right hand while staring at the monitor. Ben can tell he is in deep thought.

Bruce suddenly leans forward and stares intently at the monitor, "I can see him now!" Bruce states excitedly.

"Oh dear, I knew this would happen," Ben covers his eyes and shakes his head while leaning forward on the desk, "Bruce, if you didn't believe the story all you had to do was say so."

Bruce points at the monitor excitedly. The words are stuck in his throat, as he tries very hard to get Ben's attention.

"Not once during the story did you stop me."

Bruce shakes Ben by the shoulder.

"What Bruce!"

"L...Look at the screen," Bruce finally gets the stammer out.

Ben looks up and sees the image of Norwick glowing on the screen.

"Is th...that Norwick," Bruce asks wide-eyed.

"Glory be," Ben sits back in his chair as Bruce collapses into his. The image is bright red, and then slowly fades out, "Did you see that Bruce? That was the image of Norwick all right!"

"Yes, I...did see that," Bruce's takes a big drink of Ben's coffee, "I guess he is real then, ha," Bruce gives Ben a nervous smile and then opens the Bible, "Ah, well, ah I guess no time like the present Ben. Let's have a Bible lesson or two. What do ya say?"

Ben smiles at Bruce and pats him on the back, "Right, no time like the present," Ben laughs and scoots his chair closer to Bruce's, "Now let's see, where do we begin?"

CHAPTER 5
The Siege

The cafeteria is almost empty.

The few remaining employees gulp down coffee before rushing off to their shifts.

Two nurses sit chatting while fanning themselves with a magazine.

In the corner near the door a patient sits in his pajamas talking with his wife; glasses clang in the kitchen as the morning sun shines brightly through a wall of windows at the far end of the room.

Sharon sips on a glass of orange juice reading the morning paper a few tables down from the nurses next to the windows. Mud covers her boots, and bare legs. Her blouse and shorts soiled from sweat. In her hair hang bits of mud. She doesn't like reading the paper, and usually doesn't, but the headlines had caught her attention, "Record Heat Wave Ends." She reads down the column, then turns to the proceeding page where the article ends.

"What do they mean ends," she says aloud, realizing that her thoughts had exploded from her mouth echoing throughout the room. She smiles modestly at the staring nurses.

"Are you ok honey," asks Thelma, one of the nurses.

"Yeah, I'm just fine," Sharon says disgustingly as she leans back in her chair sipping her coffee, "Did you read this mornings headlines," she asks the heavyset African American female nurse walking toward her.

"Well, no...I didn't," Thelma walks over to Sharon's table, "...let me see here," she reaches down picking up the paper off the table. Before reading it she fans herself, "You know honey, I don't care much for the paper myself, but it sure comes in handy on days like we've been having," she smiles at Sharon, and then introduces herself, "My name is Thelma, Thelma Carter, I'm a nurse here at the hospital."

"Hi, my name is Sharon Lombardy," Sharon reaches out shaking Thelma's hand, "Glad to meet you."

"Like wise. Say, you're not from around here," Thelma looks at her while rubbing her chin, "British I'll bet?"

"No," Sharon giggles smiling wide at Thelma, "I'm from Sydney, Australia. My boss sent me to research the weather patterns in the area."

"Well, all the way from down under," Thelma smiles unfolding the paper, "Oh, this is what has you all shook up then. You don't think this heat wave is goanna to break do you?"

"No, not soon, I mean, all the data I've received hasn't shown any movement in the doom, just the cell," Sharon searches for someway to explain it.

"Doom, Cell? Honey, you've gotten me in way over my head. Listen, I don't know what the weathers like in December where you come from, but here the weather should be cold, and snowy. Doesn't even feel like Christmas."

"I know, I know and it is because of a massive doom of high pressure in the Pacific blocking the normal weather patterns all over the world. Those idiots in the paper are only placing hope where there isn't any," Sharon leans forward and sips her coffee.

"I understand dear, I think," Thelma smiles, "Maybe you need to call your boss and see if he has any news for you. Maybe, something's changed since your last update," Thelma pats Sharon on the back, "Hey, I've got to go now, relax and don't get so worked up," Thelma waves as she walks out of the Cafeteria with the other nurse.

Sharon waves, smiles then looks at her wristwatch, eleven-ten A.M. It's been over five hours since she last received a print out. She finds an electrical outlet on the far wall. As she pulls her laptop from her bag she notices Sam and Charles entering the cafeteria. She waves her hand motioning for them to join her.

"Well, it looks like you made yourself right at home," Sam smiles at Sharon.

"Yes, you see the paper has an article about the heat wave, so I'm checking it," Sharon unclips the cell phone from her belt loop and plugs in the cables leading to her laptop, "How's Charlotte?"

"The doctor said she'll be fine in a day or two. She has a sinus infection…she is tough, and has a lot of faith in that Jesus fellow. She will be just fine," Charles smiles as he sits at the table.

"Does anyone want some coffee or juice," Sam asks.

Sharon picks up her juice, shaking the carton, "Yeah, get me ones of these, thanks." Sharon says smiling.

"Wait up Sam I'll go with you. You'd think with all the running around we've done I wouldn't want to move, but I feel restless," Charles smiles at Sharon.

Sharon smiles at the two of them before returning to her laptop where she begins downloading the latest data. Appearing on her screen is a satellite picture of the US, from the Pacific side. It is a series of pictures taken at different times and then placed in a loop to make them move. The doom is breaking apart. She then clicks on a link to another satellite picture straight over the US. The cell is flattening out into a long thick line of deep blue.

"Oh, my goodness, a cold front," Sharon covers her mouth to keep from yelling.

She notices that behind the front the temperature is very cold. It is moving rapidly south out of South Dakota.

"By this time tomorrow we'll be knee deep in snow and cold. Thelma, you got your wish," she opens her e-mail program and begins typing Bruce a short message, "Call me," She sends the digital letter, and then downloads the current radar images. She finds the cold air moving in faster than she first thought.

Sam and Charles return to the table with coffee, and juice.

"So, what did that contraption tell you Sharon," Charles questions as he sits.

Sam sits across from Sharon looking at the Laptop. Still on the screen is the U.S. radar loop.

"Looks like the front is finally moving out," Sam motions to Charles to look at the screen.

"Hmm, I don't know what all that means the moving swirls and all, but it sure is interesting," Charles studies the images of swirling clouds moving in behind a blue line indicating the front.

"Yes, the Front is moving out, and those clouds you see are from the Canadian high pressure ridge that was held in check until now. The Cold air is moving in fast," Sharon looks at Charles, and then at Sam, "By this time tomorrow, we will have a very chilling experience. Charles, it looks like we got Charlotte to the hospital in time. I'd hate to see what it would be like if you were still out there in this mess," Sharon pats Charles hand as she speaks, "I truly believe that someone is looking after you, and Charlotte."

"Yeah, well you know Charlotte always had something watching over her it seems. I can't think of a time when she didn't prosper at what she did. Despite my best efforts to help her she manages to overcome," Charles smiles at Sharon, "Oh, and speaking of being watched over, Sam mentioned something about you being lead to those mounds?"

"Yes, you might not believe this, but..." Sharon and Sam explain everything to Charles, and show him the images on the laptop.

"Wholly gee! I see 'em...the image. Do you think those mounds are this place, Nicboth," Charles asks, while staring at the laptop wide-eyed, and completely astonished.

"I'm not sure," Sam sips his coffee looking at Charles, "Charles, I feel the Lord is leading Sharon and us on some sort of mission. After all, we found that old chest, and Charlotte..." Sam pauses for a moment, "Does Charlotte see things, and hear voices?"

"Well," begins Charles, "...once when our eldest son was lost she prayed for hours and hours. All us from around here went looking for him, but never did find 'em. This went on for two days. I was worried sick that some sort of foul play had taken my boy, but not Charlotte. No sir, she prayed, and prayed, until finally she came up to me and told me where the boy was. I looked at her and explained the area she wanted us to search had been covered more then once, but she insisted. She took my hand and lead me down into a dried up creek bed, and pointed under a pile of logs. Yes sir, which is where the boy was. He was covered in leaves, and was knocked out. His head was hurt very badly. He lived, and told us he was walking in the creek looking for fancy rocks when it began to rain. The water rose fast trapping him under the logs. Then when the water went down, his legs were pinned under them and he couldn't move. He hurt his head when he tried to move several logs, and one fell on him, knocking him out."

Charles sips on his coffee, "Another time, I was taken a bath and I heard her talking to someone in the bedroom. This was after the boys had grown and moved out, so we were all alone. When

I looked into the bedroom I found her on her knees looking up at the ceiling. On the bed in front of her was our Bible opened to the book of John. At first I thought she was praying, but no, she was having a conversation with someone I couldn't see. That was the only time, until this morning, that anything like that happened that I know about. Is there anything to this Jesus thing, or has Charlotte just gone plain loco," Charles looks intently at Sam, and Sharon searching their faces for some kind of answer.

"Charles, let me be the first to tell you that Jesus is alive and doing fine. As for Charlotte, I think she is sane, and that she is someone very special to him," Sam pats Charles shoulder, "I don't know if everyone has the same relationship with God as Charlotte apparently does, I know I've never heard disembodied voices or found a lost child with prayer, but I do hear, or should I say, I feel something in here," Sam points to his heart, "...that guides me, and directs my path. It is the Holy Sprit," Sam continues his testimony, and Sharon listens closely as he begins to tell of his past.

Something in his words sounds very familiar to her. In her mind she recalls a talk show where…

"Walter Gulf, you sound exactly like Walter Gulf," Sharon interrupts Sam.

Sam turns to Sharon and stammers, "Yes, well I guess I read a lot of his books, and…"

"Well, you must have memorized his books, and practiced imitating his voice, because I heard him on the radio, and you sound just like him."

"Ok, ah, well….I confess, I'm him. Walter Gulf is my pen name," Sam sits staring at Sharon.

"Why don't you just use your real name, rather than hiding behind that one," Sharon asks.

Charles sits watching this strange change of conversation.

"I was a radical, and no school is going to let a radical speak to their students, especially about evolution, but, if an intellectual were to have an opposing few of the liberal minded collegiate view then they listen. So, I changed my name and found doors opening," Sam sips some more of his coffee, and then looks gently at Sharon, "You know things are a bit different here than down under."

"You are right Sam. If this helps others understand your views then I say go for it," Sharon smiles and begins to pack her Laptop.

"Well, I hand it to ya Sam. If you can do well by being Walter Gulf, then by golly, be Walter Gulf," Charles drinks down the last of his coffee, and stands, "Are you guys ready to help me find a place to stay?"

"Charles, you and Sharon can stay with me tonight," Sam stands and pats Charles on the shoulder, "I just live right down the road."

"Sure, that will be nice, Sam…or Walter. What do you go by anyway," Sam and Sharon laugh.

* * *

The sun shines down on the summit of Nicboth. Cold wind blows sending crystals of snow from the icy peak into the thin air and against Michlu's shining armor. Silently he stands like a statue with both arms at his sides. In his mighty left hand he holds his sword. Long, sleek, and golden this instrument is symbolic in his defense of Nicboth. The true defense he knows comes from God. His eyes watch the northern horizon in anticipation. He knew this day would come, but he didn't know when. Now, he is certain that this is the time. This will be the place. The wind swirls the snow around him. His eyes loose focus as the dance catches his attention. The powdery white substance turns and twists, before the wind sends it over the peak into the crevasses below. His thoughts drift. In his mind he recalls Bel's magnificence over him.

Throughout the galaxy Bel was know as the Majestic. His honest deeds placed him at the highest ranks of God's army. Then Bel fell to Lucifer's tricks, fighting against everything he had helped to build. War was throughout Heaven, then finally Earth. The dark times came, nothing...nothing was everywhere, unfathomable blackness

Then suddenly a blast of light shown all, the galaxy destroyed. Beautiful planets left lifeless and barren. Michlu closes his eyes as tears run down his cheeks and onto the snow at his feet. He remembers Eden, and how Bel's army caught him off guard. Bel protected Lucifer as he deceived Eve, and then he watched helplessly as demons reached into their hearts and removed salvation-casting sin over them. He saw Cain and Able as children, and then he saw Able no more. He watched and protected Noah against the mobs of demons, and he watched over him as the Ark floated on the seas. He and his army protected Christ as he walked the earth, and then watched as Christ was crucified. As ordered, he did nothing to restrain the demons from doing this act to the Lord. He waited until the end of the third day and sent his angels to remove the stone, and watched in wonderment as the Christ rose. This is his strength. Christ is his power. With it nothing can stand against him.

Countless times he defended the Lords chosen against the attacks of demons, but not now. Now he protects those that haven't received the Holy Sprit, but will soon accept. The demons know them, and try to steal them away before they accept Jesus as their

Lord. Michlu and his armies watch over these saints.

He watches the movements of demons closely like he has

since the beginning. They always move in predictable patterns with sure purpose and step, but now they have employed a new tactic of stealth. They are silent, evasive, hardly showing themselves until the deed is finished, and then they scamper off to begin another.

Michlu's eyes drift back to the horizon. The snow grows heavier, and the wind blows harder on this deadly summit.

Nicboth is the fortress for angels on Earth. Here they gather to receive their orders or rest from battles which rage constantly. Lately those battles seem to be increasing, harder to win. The number of angels taking refuge here grows daily. Michlu knows that such large gatherings are dangerous. Too many angels together make them easy target for attack. He sent Scamp to Michael for re-enforcements, but he hasn't returned.

On the mountain he has three hundred angels on guard; Another thousand camped half way up, and then he has the weary, battle fatigued armies numbering in the tens of thousands scattered all over the mountain side. Such a gathering should seem imposing to Bel, but Bel has more demons on Earth than Michlu has ready armies. Michlu looks at the stars praying to God for strength, wisdom, and courage.

A trumpet blows from the west, and then another from the east. The northern trumpet blares, and then the southern. Above his head he sees a darkening mass covering the sky from horizon to horizon.

The sun is blotted out, and the wind stops blowing.

Battle trumpets blow all around Nicboth they are surrounded.

Demons taunt the guards at the base of Nicboth, but they do not move in. They hover above and stand ready all around.

Michlu shouts commands while running to the foot of the mountain to rally his troops.

"Guard, pull back, and watch the flank! Domey and Grib take your armies to the North."

angels stand with swords, staffs, and shields ready. Michlu takes the weary armies and places them in a circle, shoulder to shoulder around the mountains base. He fills in the circle with the more fatigued angels which fill the inner circle to the mountains summit.

"Gaunt Wall," he shouts, and the encircled army places their shields above their heads. Then they point their swords to the sky. At the same instance the army on the outside of the circle lifts their shield in front of them, pointing their swords to the front. The archers kneel in front taking positions above this giant pincushion, "Archers! Steady yourselves," Michlu commands.

Above him the demons bunch together in a shroud of darkness. The sky fills from one horizon to the other. Their glowing yellow eyes glare down from the sky, while they huddle together sending taunts upon the angels. The demons surrounding the base huddle in mass, stretching as far as the eye can see. Michlu watches as Python slowly descends, then stops within a few yards of Michlu.

"Hmmm looks rather familiar Michlu," Python cackles, "let's see, was it the Garden of Eden or Bethlehem? I don't remember, perhaps you can," Python arches his back laughing.

"Be gone little one," Michlu stands with his sword drawn, "and take the rest of these rebels with you!"

"You talk like you have control over us. Did you know that we have Jacobs Ladder," Michlu's eyes widen as Python continues, "Not only that, but Charlotte is dieing. She will never finish her mission," Python smiles, "Your plot is finished!" Python flutters backward while waving his sword, "Take him!"

The demons at the base begin their charge as the demons in

the air begin their decent. The ground forces step onto the mountain and immediately begin whaling in pain.

"What is happening," Python watches in horror as the ground forces vaporize into piles of ashes.

"Pull back! Pull back," Python screams.

In the air the forces meet the same fate as they reach seventy-seven feet above the mountain. Ash falls from the sky covering the angels' shields.

"Back off! Back off," Python yells while waving his arms. He glares at Michlu in rage, "This is Holy Ground! You're protected by him," Python swoops closer to Michlu, "Then why didn't I meet the fate of the others Michlu," Python's asks as eyes grow large as the revelation comes over him, "You have me trapped in here! Don't you! I can't get out," Python raises his sword above his head, "Then if I can't get out, then I will die killing you," Python dives at Michlu.

Michlu lifts his sword striking Python in the side.

Python reels in pain as he tumbles across the ground. Fe and Rumpart grab his arms, holding him out stretched in front of Michlu. Python swings his long pointed tongue at Fe, and then whips it at Rumpart.

"Hmm, this looks familiar," Michlu says while approaching the now humbled Python. "Was it at the gate, or was it during the flood? I don't recall, but I'm sure you do."

"Even though you have me trapped you'll never escape. Look above your head, and all around the mountain base. Demons are everywhere. Where are you going to go," Python laughs, then sneers at Michlu, "We'll see who last the longest."

Michlu waves his sword above his head, "Dismount!"

Immediately the angels lower their shields, and sheath their swords. Michlu begins to sing, "Oh mighty and strong God, How wonderful is your name," all the angels join him as the demons all look at one another. Python folds his ears, and vomits.

Bel arrives at the foot of the mountain in time to hear the angels praise.

"Enough," shouts Bel from the foot of the mountain. His voice as loud as thunder does not quiet the singing angels, "I said enough!"

Bel shouts once more before throwing his sword at Michlu. The razor sharp point plunges deep into Michlu's chest sending him staggering to the side.

The angels continue to sing.

Michlu steadies himself pulling the sword from his chest. He raises it along with his own sword above his head while staring at Bel. Michlu then rejoins the praise.

Bel clinches his teeth, while kicking the rocks at his feet.

"Michlu I want to talk with you," Bel demands.

Michlu continues to sing the chores to the last verse. All the angels lower to their knees to pray. The demons in the air above begin twisting and turning as the prayers ascend through them to Heaven. The mass of demons at the base turn and slowly leave.

Bel continues to taunt Michlu, "I said I want to talk with you! As soon as you're through come over here so I can...talk with you," Bel sits down on the rocky ground.

Michlu stands looking at Bel, "Do you remember Joshua," Michlu ask Bel as he carefully steps toward him, and then as Bel is about to speak Michlu continues, "Does Moses sound familiar? Does David? All of those you personally tried to destroy. Not one were you able stop! The Lord wills it and it is done! I am commanded by he who sits on high. Even your demons and your devil Lucifer proclaim him as God, you still follow him whether you like it or not! Through the darkness which you walk the Lord silently gives you the dimmest of light. You see it Bel, admit Jesus is Lord of Lords and find life again."

Michlu throws the sword to the ground at Bel's feet, then steps closer to Bel. The demons at the base who were leaving stop to watch as Michlu confronts their leader.

Bel sits on the hard ground grinding his teeth listening. His eyes fixed on Michlu.

"What do you hope to gain from following a defeated leader," Michlu asks while stepping closer.

Bel suddenly jumps to his feet, poised, ready to attack Michlu. Michlu stands his ground.

"Defeated," Bel shakes his fist stepping as close as he dares to the invisible line of Holy Ground, "You think you've won because Jesus rose from the dead! He is God! He can turn these stones into Jesus if he wanted. He can do anything, and you expect me to be impressed because he made himself rise from the dead? You think he washed away sin, and gave hope to all the men and women of Earth. He only gave them refuge and something to cling to while he makes up his next set of lies," Bel steps back and picks up a stone, "Yes, I remember David...all those songs while watching his sheep. I sent lions, and bears to attack him, and your God defended him by guiding his stones," Bel holds the stone up to Michlu squeezing it into a fine powered.

Bel pauses a moment as his mind begins to swirl, "Then some how David appears with his sling defeating my Goliath, all with Gods help," Bel staggers back a step as in his minds eye he sees himself in Heaven riding a chariot made of gold. Bels voice lowers to almost a whisper as he recalls, "Yes, I remember how I gave him Saul. I caused Saul to fall into a deep sleep, and then David didn't have the guts to kill him in that cave."

"Where was God then Bel," Michlu smiles.

"No where around him! There wasn't any angel, or anyone stopping him...he just wouldn't. He cut off a piece of garment and then the next day he showed Saul that he could have...killed him," Bel speaks slower as he contemplates what he remembers,

"Why didn't I see these things this way before? What is happening to me?"

Bels mind paints past events in a new light. He sees Gods side of the events he witnessed, "I remember Job. My army destroyed everything he owned. We took it all, and he still didn't deny the God...not one thing did he say against him," Bel lowers his head and then raises it, grits his teeth staring at Michlu, "Mind tricks...you play mind tricks with me! Yes," Bel refuses to belief what he feels is real coming from deep within himself, "God has had his victories, and we have had ours, but we give man what he truly desires! Freedom Michlu, and that's one thing you'll never be able to give them."

Bel takes a few steps back and then raises his hands toward Heaven, "Your forces are surrounded oh mighty one! Where are you to defend them? You place Holy ground at their feet, and in the air above them you make Holy as well. If these angels are yours and we are your enemy then why not let them fight," Bel stands shaking his fist at the sky, "These poor angels might get hurt, or die? So, you're their defender, Mighty God, against us? Doesn't seem fair to me. Lift your hand from them, and let us see what you made. Are these creations of a mighty God who has no reason to doubt, or are these creations the same as man, full of weakness?"

The ground begins to shake.

Boulders tumble down the mountain.

The sky above them darkens with thick bellowing storm clouds. All the angels on the mountain fall to their knees, the demons at the base of the mountain try to hide behind rocks, and those in the air try to fly, but are blown to the ground by the growing gale. Lighting flashes, thunder rumbles through the valleys surrounding Nicboth. Then the air becomes still. Everything is quite.

Bel stands defiant looking toward Heaven, and the angels continue to pray. The demons behind the rocks cautiously peek from behind them.

"Is that all you can do? Shake the ground, and blow some air," Bel shakes his fist at the sky, "Even my Lord can do that God," Bel then turns and glares at Michlu who is on his knees with his head bowed praying.

"You," Bel points his finger at Michlu, "Let me catch you outside of his protection and I'll send you back to him in pieces!"

Bel turns his back on the mountain to walk away. As he walks he waves his right arm in a circle. The demons come out from hiding to return to the mountains base and in the air above. Bel climbs up on a large boulder to stand.

"Listen to me. We came to defeat them. We will stay until we do," The demons give a loud shout and begin to taunt the angels once more, "Let me add this, these, 'angels' can not stay on this mountain forever. Stop any of them who try to escape," Bel jumps down from the boulder as the throng cheers him on.

The angels all stay kneeling in prayer.

"So still is their presence, it is like they had become rocks themselves," Python thinks as he sneaks away from Michlu joining his comrades.

* × *

Newton lies in his bed staring at the ceiling. The room is dark except for the city lights filtering through his high-rise window. He takes a long drag of his cigarette before stamping it out in the ashtray on the nightstand next to him. He watches the swirling smoke slowly glide upward then fade into the darken room. The white satin sheets lay limp across his body, and he wonders about the speech he gave that day.

In the darkness he sees two eyes glowing back at him.

"Proud of yourself today," Ce slowly growls as he sits in the darkness.

"Who are you," Newton sits up, scooting himself against the headboard, "Are you the one I was with the other night," Newton asks nervously.

"No, that was Bel, my General," Ce moves closer to the bed, where he passes thru a thin beam of light from the window. Newton watches in horror as a shiny dog like nose appears in the beam, and then a hairy snoot. As Ce's eyes move into the light Newton pushes himself up, further into the headboard. Ce's eyes are narrow, set close together like a wolf. They sink deep in the skull. Hairy eyebrows with long lashes drape across the eyes like a thin curtain. Ce continues to move closer. The light shines on a hairless forehead with two small horns protruding out of his skull above the pointed ears. The rest of the head is hairless. The skin, wrinkled with a deep gray color. The yellow eyes float through the darkness to the foot of his bed. Newton can hear a low growl like a cat purring, but more intense and deep. Newton's heart races as he watches the eyes move along the edge of the mattress closer to him. Ce stops his advance at the nightstand.

"Weak, pathetic human," Ce whispers.

Newton now pushes himself to speak. With every bit of strength he moves his trembling lips, "Just what is it you want?" Newton then pulls the satin sheet up to his chin to hide himself.

Ce growls softly, turns his back to Newton before circling to the foot of the bed.

"Listen to me," Ce speaks so soft that Newton strains to hear, "You're only a piece of a puzzle that started years ago. Long before there was a United States," Ce growls loader and begins to speak sharply. He jumps up on the bed moving close to Newton placing his dog like nose inches from the Senators face. Newton feels the hot stench of Ce's breath, "Before there was a Christ a motion was set in place that you are just now a part of. What do I want," Ce chuckles then jumps off the bed walking into the shadows. In the darkness he turns and faces Newton again, "The speech you gave today was good, but if I didn't have an army of demons helping you Senator, you would have been a laughing stock. Most humans don't believe in Global Warming. It is up to us to convince them that it is real and that the situation is worse than it really is....Fear Senator, fear is the key," Ce stands on his hind legs above Newton with his hands on his hips. He glares down at the Senator who cowards beneath his sheets, "You're no different than any human. You lie, and will do anything for power," Ce hops off the bed sitting on the floor next to the bed. Newton pulls the sheets down below his eyes, peeking out to survey the room, "Come out from under there so I can speak with you. Even your President doesn't gravel the way you do.

Newton slowly pulls the sheets down and sits up, "Do you mean the...."

"Yes, the President. You have an appointment with him in the morning, I arranged it. He is a piece of the puzzle too," Ce slowly turns away walking off.

"Wait," Newton yells. Ce turns growling loudly. Newton sinks back into the bed pulling the sheets up to his chin, "You said you were going to tell me something," Newton stammers. Ce turns slowly around.

"It will wait until you're with the President. That way you both will hear it together," Ce turns back into the darkness. Newton watches as the figure steps further in the shadows. As Ce's disappears behind a curtain of darkness he notices his cigarette stub still smoldering in the ashtray,

"Time is nothing to these creatures," he says aloud.

CHAPTER 6
Secrets

Bone chilling wind rushes into Missouri freezing the hard dry earth turning the rain drenched areas into lakes of ice. Those who survived the drought, and others who survived the floods, now must hurry to seal their houses from the Northern invasion of arctic air now blasting in from Canada. Snow swirls from darkened clouds, which once produced torrents of rain. Whiteout conditions all over the mid-west strand many leaving some to the fate of the freezing cold.

Sam builds a fire in his fireplace, while Charles enters the room with an armload of firewood. Sharon sits in a chair typing an email she hopes will get some kind of response from Sam, or Bruce. She hasn't heard from them all day. Sam generously donated some old winter clothes to Charles and Sharon. The clothes fit Charles loosely, but hang like sacks on Sharon. The wind howls through the surrounding woods causing Sharon to stop typing and listen.

"Is that wolfs," she whispers to Sam.

"No, it's the wind blowing past the rough bark of those Pine and Oak trees out there," Sam smiles at Sharon, "You do have winter down under don't you?

"Yes, but it isn't at all like this. Listen, I've read about those wild timber wolfs, bears, and the like you Americans have roaming around your country side."

Charles drops another armload of wood in the holder startling Sharon.

"Sorry, didn't mean to frighten ya, but as far as bears, and wolfs you have nothing to worry about. This is Missouri, not Montana, or some of those northwestern states. The meanest thing you'll find here is a black bear, but their more afraid of you than you of them. The next thing is coyotes, and you won't find many of them. Now, wild dogs and maybe an occasional Cougar deep in the Ozarks, nothing worth frighten over. Wolf's....that's a long shot, haven't been one reported around here in years, not to say one might wonder in from time to time," Charles places a few more chunks of wood on the fire, and smiles again at Sharon.

Sharon takes comfort in Charles explanation, but as the wind howls outside holds her doubts.

"Hey, why don't we look into the chest you two found and see what all this is all about," Charles suggest.

"Sounds good to me, I carried it in while you two were getting cleaned up. It's sitting in the corner over there," Sam points to the dirty trunk sitting in the corner next to his gun rack and fishing poles. Sharon places her laptop on the coffee table, while Sam and Charles carry the large olive green trunk from near the fireplace.

Dust covers the trunk with bits of leaves hanging from old cobwebs. Sam wipes the trunk clean with a rag as Sharon finds the latch and opens the lid.

The wind becomes suddenly still.

Inside the trunk lay large bulging manila envelopes, along with about a dozen gray matchbox size boxes. Charles removes the boxes and envelopes handing them to Sharon who stacks them on a large dinning table a few feet away. Sam stands at the table counting the envelopes then sorting them by the big red number printed on them. Charles then discovers a shinny black box about two feet long and four inches wide. It has brass hinges. Engraved on the lid is a swastika.

Like a statue, he kneels staring at the shinning black box, "What in the world is this," Charles reaches in lifting the box out, finding two more underneath identical to the first. As he removes the third black box, a small red box dislodges from underneath the envelopes tumbling to the floor of the chest.

The bellowing winter clouds disperse as a bright winter sky fills with stars.

Charles picks up the red box holding it as if he were looking at a diamond. The small case is smooth and shinny. The lid, held tight by a gold lock clasp. An eagle is engraved on the lid with its wings spread. He slowly pushes the clasp to open it.

"What's that," Sharon asks startling Charles, "I'm sorry I didn't mean to frighten you."

"That's ok, I found this neat looking box, and was about to open it," Charles holds the box out for Sharon to see.

"Wow that is neat. Go ahead, open it and let's see," Sharon watches closely as Charles loosens the clasp then slowly pushes the lid open with his thumb. As the lid rises Sharon's eyes grow wide. The lifting lid reveals a sparkling red ruby sitting nestled on a red pillow, "Oh, my goodness," Sharon whispers.

Red shooting stars streak across the winter sky.

"I never saw anything like this before," Charles gazes at the ruby's brilliance before snapping the lid shut. He turns looking at Sharon who is still staring transfixed at the box, "Sharon, we need to turn this stuff over to someone. I mean all this just doesn't make any since."

"I know, but we were meant to find it Charles. There is a reason why all this is happening," Sharon slowly removes the box from Charles hand carrying it over to the table placing it with the rest of the things from the trunk.

Demons, Strumpet and Caldor stand in the woods near Sam's house. Although some distance away they watch Sharon through the window as she places the red box on the table. Strumpet signals his squad to move closer.

Sol stands alone next to the fireplace feeling the demon movements. He knows he will not get reinforcements, but he doesn't care. Before Michlu left for Nicboth he told Sol this would happen. Sol remembers, "God gives you charge over these three. If he gives you charge then you should stand fast for his strength is with you," Sol drops to his knees and thanks God. His ears hear the fluttering of wings above his head and the pawing of claws on the roof. All his senses come alive as he reaches his hand toward Heaven, "What is your will oh Lord? Should I smash them casting their green dust into the wind? Should a cut them to shreds leaving not even the smallest remnant? Tell me I pray Lord, and I will do it, I'm your servant, not one of those rebels."

The demon squad stops their advance toward the house.

"You there," Caldor yells at a small demon that is shaking and backing away from the house, "Why are you stopping?"

The demon points towards the house, "You don't feel it do you? The power of God is in there," the little demon turns flying into the night. Soon, others follow the little demons lead.

Strumpet and Caldor lift their swords turning toward the house. After a few steps they begin to feel the wrath of Gods anger. As if arms made of fire have wrapped around them, squeezing tightly. The wrath turns hot, burning them. Sol stands in front of them.

"Go," Sol shouts thunderously.

The hot wrap falls from them freeing them to fly away.

Charles removes the remaining envelopes from the trunk before joining Sam and Sharon at the table, "Well that's the last of it," he says then as he sets the packages on the table he feels something strange, "What in tar nations is that," he rubs the back of his neck, and then his arms.

Sam and Sharon stop and look at Charles who is standing at the far end of the table looking out the Window and rubbing his arms. They look toward the window and see nothing, but darkness.

Charles looks at them puzzled, "Don't you feel it?"

"Yes, I do feel something," Sharon begins rubbing the back of her neck and then her arms. She closes her eyes and feels warmth inside her as she has never felt before. She suddenly opens her eyes. Now, for the first time in many days she feels relaxed and less tense. She is completely consumed with a feeling of contentment as she sits in the wooden chair at the table.

"What happened just now," Sharon asks.

"The Lord is watching over us Sharon. I feel that there is something on this table that the Lords enemies do not want reveled," Sam begins to open an envelope. Sharon and Charles both do the same. Sam stops to pray, "Oh Lord guide our thoughts, and our hands as we search for whatever you have for us to find," Then he reaches into the envelope. In it he finds charts and graphs with a lot of writing on them in German.

Sharon finds more of them in her envelope.

Charles finds papers with a list of names. Charles sheets have an additional attached sheet translation to English.

"Oh, these names are Jewish, and these dates are all during the war," Charles ruffles through the stack of papers, "These must be....no. They couldn't! Why," He looks at Sharon, "These are the names of the Jews from the holocaust I bet. Look at them. He hands the list to Sharon. Look at the names, the dates, and the cities. Look in the far right column it has the names of concentration camps where they were taken."

Sharon stares at the list, "Sam, look at this. He's right! What is all this doing in a trunk way out here in St. Charles County."

Sam takes a look at the papers and then hands his manila envelope to Charles, "You're right, but look at this Charles. I started with envelope one. The papers inside indicate the formulas are from Munich. Found by the First American Infantry after a very bloody battle. It seems the Germans had plans for a bomb greater than the atomic bomb. These first few pages describe it, and how they were going to use it. Now, the list you have is not a list of Jews who were sent to the camps, but they are a list of Jews that left Germany before the holocaust, and what camps they were to be sent to if they were captured. According to the second page there should be another list indicating the places those same Jews migrated to after leaving Germany. The bomb was to be used on those cities they moved to," Sam shuffles the remaining pages around, "All of this needs to be looked at real close and examined before we hand it over to anyone."

"Why weren't these destroyed Sam," Sharon asks turns to Sam, "They might not have wanted them discovered at that time, but they also didn't want them destroyed. What is so important about this little bit we discovered so far anyway. Plans for a bomb, Yes, but why wasn't that put somewhere safe? A list of names of refugees, and Hitler's plans to kill them...It doesn't make any since to me why someone would go through all of this trouble to hide this kind of information."

"Yes, I agree, and I think we need to do as Sam says and start digging," Charles picks up another envelope.

"This might take a while," Sharon says opening another envelope."

"Yep, and I'll put a pot of coffee on for us," Sam adds.

Sharon watches Sam leave from the kitchen looking over at Charles who is busy looking into another envelope. Then she looks at the pile of articles from the chest and thinks about the voice from the tape. She isn't sure now if the voice was telling her to go to Nicboth.

* * *

"Ok, quit pushing me already, I'm awake," Bruce grumbles as Ben wakes him.

"It's about time you woke up. The sun's been up for a couple of hours now. We need to get moving," Ben grabs his backpack filling it with his cooking utensils, and dirty clothes.

Bruce sits up, stretches. He looks above his head at the smooth roof of the rock overhang they had slept under, "This was a great idea, Ben. I slept like a log."

"I know and you snored like it too. Now come on, get a move on we have a hike ahead of us," Sam finishes filling his bag then hands Bruce his breakfast.

Bruce turns towards Ben just in time to see his breakfast on a stick, "What in the world is that," Ben pushes the stick a little closer to Bruce, "I'm supposed to eat that," Bruce quickly jumps out of bed, backing away while holding his hands out in front of him, "I'm not eating that thing."

Ben stops his advance holding the lizard on a stick up to his nose, "Sure smells good. Kind of reminds me of chicken."

"Sure, everything smells like chicken, then you bite into it and it taste like two week old road kill," Bruce spits, then turns away as Ben begins to eat the lizard.

"I didn't think you would eat it anyway. There's some dry milk and a bag of dry cereal in the nap sack over there. Mix the milk with water from the spring and it's almost like store bought. Let's hurry we have one more day of hiking ahead of us," Sam takes another bite of the lizard, then holds it up to Bruce, "Got you out of bed with it didn't I," Ben smiles, as Bruce prepares his milk at the stream.

"Do you think Sharon will miss us, I mean we didn't even tell her we were leaving, for that matter we didn't tell anyone," Bruce asks while he prepares his cereal.

"You know Bruce; I believe Norwick was calling to me, not Sharon," Ben says as he sits down near the fire.

"Yeah, but still, shouldn't we contact someone and tell them where we're going?"

"Would they believe us, 'Oh, by the way Sharon, we are going to Nicboth. Don't bother calling us.'"

"Do you think that demon Norwick, was calling to you?"

"Yes, Bruce, I really do."

"So, this place Nicboth, where is it exactly?"

"I'm taking you to a place that holds many wonders and gives one a since of being. Nicboth is near there I'm sure, and possibly an answer to all of this," Ben slings the backpack onto his shoulders, "If you don't get moving it will be nightfall before we get there, and believe me, you don't want to be caught where we are going after dark."

"Ok, I'm coming…." Bruce stops and looks at Ben, "What do you mean by that, 'don't want to be caught,' is someone chasing us, or will there be," Bruce stands nervously looking at Ben.

"Well, there isn't anyone chasing us now, but who knows, when we get there it is possible," Ben picks up his canteen, and begins to march down the trail, "So, come on we are losing day light."

"Ben, wait," Bruce picks up his pack and runs down the trail toward Ben spilling milk from his bowl as he runs.

* * *

The sun glistens on the snow as the wind swirls through the Pine Forest of Nicboth. Here on the lower slopes Michlu kneels in prayer, as Bel lies back on a large boulder a short distance from the invisible border.

"Angels, what do they know? You don't even know this Jesus you worship," Bel grumbles at Michlu, "I bet you don't even know what he has done to deserve the praises of those humans you're trying to protect," Bel stands kicking the dirt at his feet.

Above them demons swirl in a black mass like a thousand sparrows before migration. This black mass spins twirls, then twist shaping and reshaping itself as it glides. Michlu stands watching this as he stretches. Then he turns away from Bel walking towards the summit.

"Where are you going," Bel shouts while jumping off the rock, "Come back here and fight," Bel grits his teeth, growling. With his fist clinched he begins kicking the stony earth. The commotion wakens the sleeping mass of demons and they hurry to his aid.

Michlu continues walking.

"Where is he going," ask De, a demon like Python.

"He is going where God tells him to go," snarls Bel, "Take Wit and Smuka with you and watch him. Do not let him out of your site," Bel barks as he picks up De by the neck, "Don't do like you did at Calvary, do you hear me!"

"Yes," gasps De, "It won't happen again," as Bel loosens his grasp, De flutters off to find Wit and Smuka.

* * *

"There it is, Bruce," Sam points to the top of a large rocky slope, "See that Rock that looks like an egg on the right?"

"Yes, I see it. Is that where we are going to camp tonight," Bruce shakes off his pack and takes a long drink from his canteen.

"Both, now don't drag your feet and let's get moving," Ben smiles at Bruce and turns to continue the march.

"Didn't I ask you to stop doing that Ben? You're driving me crazy with that, 'Both' business," Bruce slings his pack on his back running to catch up with Ben, "Hey, wait up."

The dry hill country provides very little shade. What shade there is comes from sparsely leafed trees, or from large boulders. The slope is different from the rest of the desert. It has a spattering of trees, and the trail is dirt instead of sharp flint rock. Bruce's boots slip every few steps as he tries desperately to keep up with Ben who climbs the steep incline steadily. As the trail draws closer to the egg shaped boulder it levels off and opens into a large clearing walled by larger boulders. Bruce and Ben stand in the middle of this arena resting.

"What is this place," Bruce asks, "Looks a like a good place to camp," Bruce notices Ben shocked expression at his statement.

"No, we aren't spending the night in this spot. We would be dead by morning," Ben smiles again at Bruce placing his hand on his shoulder, "This, my boy, is Holy Ground to the Aborigine."

"What, you didn't mention…I thought you said, 'Both,' while ago, and now your telling me…explain to me again why we are here," Bruce takes off his backpack, and turns to speak again only to find Ben marching off, "Hey, wait a minute…I'm not taking another step... Ben wait," Bruce trots up to Ben grabbing him by the arm, "Wait Ben lets talk."

"Ok...we can talk here and let them have our skins, or we can get out of their temple and talk over there where they don't care if you sit all day, or camp," Ben points to the tops of the boulders at native Aborigine men standing looking down at them.

Bruce's eyes grow large.

"Now which do you prefer," Ben asks as Bruce pushes past him hurrying up the trail. Ben chuckles, "I was only kidding, don't hurry so fast. They won't harm us," Ben laughs.

Ben's pleadings were too late. Bruce was already far up the trail and rounding a bin. He hurries across the dust-laden trail, and then stops abruptly at the foot of a tall rock. The boulder is immensely rounded. Its smooth sides cascade upward to a rounded point giving it the shape of an egg.

"This sure didn't seem this big from way down there? Ben...where are you," Bruce turns to find Ben already past him kneeling quietly beside a tree, "Ben are you all right," he steps closer and realizes Ben is praying, "Oh, sorry! I didn't understand," Bruce quietly kneels besides Ben.

"This is a grave of a very precious man to me," Ben speaks softly with his head still bowed, "The man buried here is my father."

Bruce slowly raises his head looking understandingly at his trail boss.

"This is one of the reasons I brought you here," Ben raises his head and stands while speaking, "The man in this grave is my earthly father. He no longer hears, sees, speaks, or breathes. What I say at this grave will never reach his consciousness, because he no longer has any, but one day my Heavenly father will come and these bones in the ground will burst fourth with flesh. Jesus will raise him from the dead," Ben turns and takes a few steps away before removing his pack and sits down under a shady bush. Bruce stares down at the well-kept grave. The head stone is clean and the mound of dirt covering the grave is smooth and rounded. "The Aborigines loved my father, and keep his grave in better condition than they do their own loved ones," Ben opens his pack retrieving a small black book.

"What's that," Bruce walks closer to Ben.

"This is one of my father's diaries, his last one. He kept details of everything he found out here in the bush for the Australian Ecological Society, but he also kept notes in this book of personal observations," Ben taps the rough brown cover, "In this book is a map leading to Nicboth."

"Nicboth! Why didn't you tell me this earlier," Bruce asks dumbfounded.

"Yes, you see my father use to tell me stories about a place where angels gather to rest and worship. I always thought the stories were some sort of fairy tale, but when Norwick told Sharon to go to Nicboth I knew my fathers' stories were real," Ben opens the book and quickly leafs to a page containing a map, "I don't know why I never thought of it before. Look at the start of the map," Ben points to the page and then to the egg shaped rock, "...there is the start of our journey to Nicboth."

* * *

"Yes Mr. President, right away," An aid turns smartly in an about face marching from the Presidents desk. Entering the executive corridor, he turns to a bench where guest wait for their visitations with the President of the United States. Alone on the bench is Senator Newton.

The President will see you now Senator," the aid informs the Senator.

"Yes, thank you," Newton nervously stands then approaches the entrance, "Is there anyone with him?"

"No, you will be completely alone as the President has ordered," the aid answers.

"Good, thank you again," Newton steps into the Oval Office as the aid closes the door behind him. Newton's nervousness is apparent as he slowly makes his way to the desk. The President is sitting at the desk reading Newton's report he gave to the Senate.

"Very interesting," the President taps a pencil on the desk as he reads, "...the waters of the world will rise nearly eighty feet. New Orleans and the entire Mississippi Valley will be under water, including St. Louis, and most of St. Charles County, Missouri," he lays the report on the desk and looks intently at Newton who is standing in front of the desk like a schoolboy about to be reprimanded, "Oh, where are my manners, please sit down," he points to a chair in front of the desk. Newton stumbles as he sits, then sits rigidly, with a blank stare on his face. "Stop worrying. I won't bite you," the President offers him a cigar, but Newton refuses.

"Irritates my throat," Newton's forces the words out.

The President places the cigars case on the desk then gazes at Newton a long while before speaking, "This report is good. Most people understand the earth is warming, but refuse to believe these alarmist theories. It is not the habit of this administration to cover the, butt of Senators. Furthermore, it is not my business to endorse such cheap tricks in swaying the vote of Senators or Congressmen, however, I like it as it does set a tone my administration can work with...good job."

Newton's heart races.

The President continues, "If it wasn't for Que you would not be in this office today sitting before me like a wincey school boy, show some backbone Senator, relax. I've went the proverbial, 'extra mile' and enhanced your report, removing some of your exaggerations. You were right about one thing…If the ice caps melt St. Charles County will mostly be under water."

Newton slowly releases the tight grip on the armrest.

"…and if it is, then we must rescue a certain article we have hidden there," the President finishes.

"Article?"

"Well, a box containing some items from Hitler's debacle."

"Hitler's what?"

"Relax, take it easy. Que will explain everything to you."

The Presidents watches as Newton lets out a breath that he held since entering the office.

"That's better. Now, I know you've been through a lot the last couple of months, and when Bel first came to me I thought I had gone mad. Even went around mumbling to myself a few times. Remember, they placed me in the hospital for a day or two," the President laughs.

Newton nods.

"While I was in the hospital an old friend came to me and explained everything quit clearly. You see the Christians are fooled just like the Jews in believing in only one God. Why, we are all Gods you know. Que showed you that in the cave."

Newton remembers the colored dancing flames, and the images, "Yes, yes I do remember. He said we are all Gods of our own dominions. He will give this all to us, everything the Jews refused from him, and he will give to those who follow him. We are Gods! Besides, Adam was God…we are his decedents making us Gods," Newton's entire disposition transforms. He is now leaning forward in his chair wide eyed, excited, full of a renewed energy.

The lights flicker and then go out.

Cold air fills the room.

The President watches a shadow move in the darkness to his desk.

Newton watches the same shadow, but is not scared any longer.

CHAPTER 7
Disclosure

Glowing red cinders smolder beneath the last flicker of flame in the fireplace. Sam looks at Sharon sleeping on the coach, then at Charles who is nestled in the recliner. Earlier he had brought them blankets and tended to the fire. It seemed like only minutes, but by the fire he knew it had been hours. He glances at the clock on the wall, Five A.M. Crossing the room to the fireplace he places several more logs on the smoldering flame. Returning to the table he sits looking at all the envelopes.

He then notices the gray matchbox size boxes stacked neatly where Charles was sitting. He checks Charles list to see if had looked at them. He had not. He picks one up placing it in his palm. Holding it under the table light he examines it closer. The box is gray, with a flip top lid, no markings. He opens the box slowly. Inside he finds the box lined with a soft tissue paper folded crisply over the main contents. The paper is sealed tight with glue. Sam doesn't want to rip it. With his sharp pocketknife he carefully slices between the folds through the glue. Then he gently opens the folds. Sam sits the box down still looking into it.

"This is impossible. How could this be here, and why is it in this collection…it just couldn't be," Sam thinks to himself.

He places a clean sheet of paper on the table. The book fits snug inside the matchbox causing Sam to take extra precautions to avoid ripping the box or book. Sam lifts the book out by the tissue paper carefully sitting it on the sheet folding the paper down around it. The book is very primitive with thin leather strips ran through holes on one edge at the top and bottom and then tied off making a loop creating its binding. The front and back covers are made from thin pieces of leather. On the front cover is the title, "Omega I."

"The Omega."

Sam has heard of these books, but never thought they actually existed.

"What are you mumbling about over there," Sharon says while sitting up on the coach, squinting her eyes to see.

"Sorry for waking you, I didn't realize I was talking out load."

"Oh, it wasn't you. The fire is hot and that woke me. What do you have there," Sharon gets up from the coach and sits at the table.

"You won't believe this. This could be an ancient book from the Middle East written by Henicky on the Island of Redi. I haven't opened the book yet to see if it is or isn't…."

"Now wait a minute," Sharon wipes some sleep from her eyes, "You mean, 'the,' Henicky?"

"Yes, the legend has it that before his death he wrote twelve books, each revealing the secret testimonies of Roman, and Jewish leaders about the life of Christ," Sam points to the stack of gray boxes on the table.

"Really, and you think these are the books," Sharon picks up one of the boxes, "Awfully small books."

"He wrote them small so he could hide them from the

Romans. What I can't figure out is why these books are in this trunk with the rest of this stuff."

Sam picks up the small book and carefully thumbs through it.

"I can tell you why," Sam and Sharon turn to Charles as he stretches and stands up from the recliner, "That Hitler wanted all sorts of things. Do you think he wanted Africa for control of the Mediterranean, or the Arab nations for the oil? No way, that was his excuse for invading them. He was after the Ark containing the Ten Commandments. You know that movie wasn't to far off. Hitler wasn't interested in the commandments, but the power of the Ark. Remember how the Hebrews carried it into battle before them, and they couldn't loose. Hitler thought the same thing would happen to his Army. With the ark they would rule the world, or at least that's what he thought," Charles takes a chair opposite of Sam, "Those little books you found," Charles points at them, "if they are what you say they are then Hitler wanted to hide those testimonies from the world."

Sam thumbs through the book he removed, "These books, as the legend has it, were hidden by a group of Henicky's followers. Several times through the ages men have tried to find them, but always ill fate found them first."

"I read that too in an old book on myths and legends," Sharon says while opening the last envelope.

Charles picks up one of the small boxes and examines it while Sam continues leafing through the small book. He looks at Sharon who is holding a piece of ruffled paper while looking into the envelope, "What did you find?"

"Oh, this rough looking letter written in German and nothing else really, except this," Sharon holds up another sheet of paper with the Department of Defense logo on the top and a big red, "Top Secret" stamped across its middle. She looks at the letter,

"It was written on, December 13, 1945, by the Department of Defense, and it reads,

> *'The articles contained, here in, are of the utmost secrecy and for special, "A" class personal. The letter was found in Berlin on, April 30th, 1945 by an advance American patrol. They snuck through German defenses ahead of the Russian advance, to secure the safe liberation of seven German officers being held as traitors by the German authority. It was vital these men make it out alive as they held testimony of war crimes against many ranking German officials. However, the patrol made it to the prison immediately after the Germans executed these men. After a thorough search of the area, and the slain men, they found a letter in the hand of Field Marshal, Baron Von Basin; he was the ranking officer of the seven. This letter of confession states theses men were collaborators with Hitler in plotting and exterminating of the Jews from Poland. It also names two generals as giving them the orders to perform these acts.'"*

"Wholly Smokes! That letter should be in a museum instead of in an old trunk," Sam barks.

"Wait," Sharon asks, "…there's more. They interpreted the letter.

> *To the victors, may Gods grace always be with you and never leave you. It is my regret to have been a part of this war machine. My hands are stained with the blood of all we have murdered. The demons came from everywhere deceiving us and planting seeds of pride and nationalism. How I wish I did not listen and let them do their worst to me then, but I, like all the rest yielded to their desires for we feared them more than God.*

The Fuehrer and his closest staff hold to them as if they were the means of life. We are Guilty. When we brought the Jews from Poland, we laughed, kicked and poked them, nothing was better to torture. We left most in the camps, and we brought about twenty to Berlin and we did what we pleased with them; children, young men, and women, and old women...no one was immune. Generals Dammil, and Ghersh ordered us to take the children away—get rid of them. When we went into the cells to chase them out they were already dead, dead of malnutrition. That was the first time a came close to crying and began seeing things differently and the beast knew it. The demons taunted me and came to my room as I slept. Even now as I write this they stand near the bars and spit at me. To all these things I am guilty, and deserve what fate God has for me.

*Field Marshal
Baron Von Basin'"*

Sharon sits motionless holding the letter. Sam stares at her as if hoping for more.

Charles sits looking down at the tabletop, unusually quite.

"That's it....I guess this guy was crazy...demons and all," Sharon places the letter back in the envelope then looks at Sam, "Right then, he has to be crazy...right."

Sam holds up the Omega, "I don't know. It does sound a bit far fetched, but look at all these things...a ruby, the small books, maps, formulas, that letter....all of these things are related somehow. Why would anyone hide this stuff? That is the real puzzle."

"Now hold on," Charles looks up from the table, "...you haven't heard everything. You both are too young to remember much about World War Two and what you do know you read in history books, or saw in the movies, I was there."

"You were there," Sharon asks as she turns toward Charles.

"Yes, I was in Berlin and saw a great many things I wish to forget."

Sam places his hand on Charles shoulder, "You don't have to talk about it if you don't want to."

"Oh, well...I guess it won't hurt anything if I tell ya," Charles begins, "I was a Sergeant in the Second Armor division, Bravo Company, Assault Team Foxtrot was the lead assault tactical unit and it was divided into four squads. My squad was the lead squad on most combat missions. It also had the highest mortality rate of any squad in the European arena. I saw more death than most men because we were always the first in and the last out of most battles. Now, being an armor unit you think we would have a tank or some other type of armor back up. This wasn't the case, we were lead, meaning we went ahead and scouted out the locations of enemy troops, and sent coordinates for artillery barrages, or tank assaults. This placed us in very vulnerable positions most of time. I lost track of how many such missions we went on, but I can count on my hand the number of times we didn't loose someone to enemy attacks, three." Charles bows his head.

"Sounds like you were one of the lucky ones," Sharon hands Charles a cup of coffee.

"Lucky? That depends on what you consider luck. Anyway, on April fifth-tenth, nineteen-forty-five, Bravo Company was just outside of Berlin and my squad was given the order to go into the city and liberate seven men. Those ones mentioned in that there letter...I was the one that found that letter."

"Man, this is incredible," exclaims Sam.

"Yes, what are the chances of you and this letter being this close together after all these years, and not only that for many years, it was just down the road from your farm...simply incredible, indeed," Sharon smiles at Charles, then sees a tear rolling down Charles cheek.

"After finding the letter," Charles continues, "I folded it and placed in my shirt pocket. We were in a hurry to get out of the area because Russian mortar shells were landing all over the place and the Germans were still fighting hard. A mortar round killed three of my men and a Russian machine gun took care of the other five. I laid low near a pile of debris. The Russians ran past me and I skedaddled back to my unit as fast as I could. I gave the letter to my commander never knowing what it said, until now. There is one thing you both need to remember, Hitler and most of his staff were into the occult. They had mediums, and all sorts of advisors that were occultist. You also need to remember that the Arians thought they were supreme to everyone, and that anyone that wasn't an Arian was low life, plain trash."

"Charles, I'm sorry you had to go through all that," Sharon reaches across the table and pats Charles hand.

Charles looks into Sharon's eyes as tears roll down his cheeks, "Yes, war isn't the glamorous stuff you see on TV...to quote General Sherman, *'War is Hell!'*"

* * *

Snow swirls at Michlu's feet as he steadily marches to the mountaintop of Nicboth. De, Wit, and Smuka fly safely overhead watching every step Michlu takes.

Michlu stops at the summit looking out over the majestic beauty surrounding him. His eyes swell with tears as he is overcome with joy, "Your creation, oh Lord, is great," he shouts, "Who am I to defend you? With one word you can destroy it all, and I cannot even melt this snow. It is by your power, by your strength, and by your will alone that I exist. What is your will Lord," Michlu then falls to his knees and prays.

"He is lost," De whispers to Wit.

"No, he is forsaken! The Lord has not responded to his prayers for help, and he feels abandon," Wit snickers drawing his sword.

"Shall we attack him while he is helpless?" Smuka says, also drawing his sword preparing for the onslaught.

"Wait, both of you! You didn't learn anything from Calvary," De circles in front of them stopping their advance, "We thought the Son of Man had given up too, remember?"

Wit and Smuka look at each other nodding approvingly at De.

"We lost thousands because he was still protected. Those angels were all around him as he uttered his last words, 'It is finished,' but we didn't see them. As we moved in they pounced on us. Now, do you really want that to happen again," De asks, glaring to his brothers.

"What do we do then? Fly around up here and just watch," Smuka pushes De aside, "You might be afraid, but I'm not! That is not the Son of Man down there," Smuka arches his back stretching his wings as he dives toward Michlu.

De and Wit watch helplessly knowing he will not reach his goal. Smuka realizes this too, but has gone too far, and to fast to pull out of his dive. The invisible barrier consumes him. As Smuka passes through he is instantly devoured. All that remains is his falling ashes over the white snow below.

"Warnings are not enough for some," De smiles at Wit. Both let out an eerie cackle then return to watching Michlu.

Michlu stands, "Yes Lord, I will obey and trust in you. I will watch over them," Michlu turns from the summit to a small outcrop of rocks on the lower portion of the mountain where Bel can see him clearly. De and Wit flutter down to Bel.

"Well, what's your report," Bel barks at De.

"He prayed and then announced he would watch over them, but he didn't say who," De reports.

"Yes, and then he walked to that group of rocks," Wit adds.

"There has to more to this," Bel approaches the invisible boundary again shouting to Michlu, "Have you been given charge over rocks," Bel's army laughs at his mockery, "Come on over here and fight me," Bel taunts.

* * *

Bruce reaches carefully into Ben's backpack trying not to wake Ben who is sleeping close by. The tightly knotted nylon string makes it difficult to open, but Bruce manages to undo the bowline, and flip the pocket open. Silently he pulls the diary from the pocket.

"I don't think he will mind if I thumb through this," Bruce thinks to himself as he gives the book a finale tug.

Quickly he ducks under his blanket turning on his flashlight. Before he can begin though, Ben yank's the blanket off him.

"What are you doing," Ben stands over Bruce with his hands on his hips.

"You said I could read it, and I didn't want to wake you, Ben. Honest, I was curious that's all," Bruce explains while standing.

"It's alright Bruce," Ben laughs, "you just looked awfully funny sitting there in the dark with that blanket over your head and that flashlight," Ben walks over to the fire throwing a couple of sticks onto it.

"Boy, you gave me a fright, Ben," Bruce walks over to the fire sitting close to where Ben is kneeling placing large sticks on the fire, "It is alright isn't it, I mean to read this?"

"Sure, I thought you would, or at least I hoped you would. Did you get any sleep," Ben looks at the horizon where the suns first rays are stretching across the morning sky onto long cigar shaped clouds.

"Yes, I slept like a baby, but I started thinking about the diary and Nicboth. Do you really think we can find it?"

"Yes I do. The map shows a trail leading beyond the Egg Rock into a cave. I haven't explored that cave and the Aborigine will not go into it. They say it is Holy."

"A cave! We are going into a cave that you know nothing about?"

"Yes, we will take all the necessary precautions, but if it bothers you, you don't have to go. I do not want you to if you're not willing. You can stay here with the Aborigine."

"Oh, that's ok. I'll go with you," Bruce stands and begins packing his gear.

"What are you doing," Ben chuckles.

"We might as well get started, or do you want to cook me another lizard," Bruce smiles at Ben.

"Both," Ben smiles.

The sun is barely over the horizon as they find the entrance to the cave obscured with large rocks and brush. A thin trail leads the two through to the dark abyss. The entrance is reveled after they squeeze between two boulders. They stand looking down into the mouth of darkness. Directly in front of them is a steep incline funneling to a narrow dark passage. Bruce picks up a fist size rock throwing it into the dense blackness. Silence for a moment, then the sharp crisp clatter of the stone striking against a surface equally as hard. Ben clicks on his flashlight revealing a rough carpet of sharp flint rock on the slope. At the bottom jagged stone points protruding from the entrance walls.

"You first," suggest Bruce.

Ben looks at Bruce and smiles. He then ties off a rope to a large boulder lowering himself. The sharp flint rock slides easily under his boots as he slowly descends. His flashlight dangles from the hook on his belt sends its beams in all directions as Ben slides safely to the opening.

"Great! I guess it's my turn now," Bruce yells down the fifty-foot embankment.

"No, wait! I want to look things over first," Ben shines his light around the rough opening, then into the dark confines beyond.

"The opening looks large enough for us to fit through. Beyond that is a long narrow corridor…we can slip through it."

"Ok then, here I come," Bruce slides down to the opening. Not as smooth as Ben though. His heels catch on an embedded stone sending him head over heels until Ben catches him.

"Are you all right Bruce?"

"Yes, I think so. Outside of a few scratches I should be alright," Bruce stands brushing himself off, "How long is the corridor?"

"I'm not sure, but we're going to find out."

The corridors rough narrow sides, and low ceiling cause Ben and Bruce to walk hunched over. The flashlight beams cast ghostly shadows down the corridor ahead of them. To Bruce the shadows seem to be alive as they dart behind rocks, disappear, and then reappear, this adds to his nervousness. The two walk carefully and silently. The only sound comes from the rough grinding of their boots on the wet cave floor and the occasional distinct drip of water echoing from some place ahead. The air is damp and cold, but they seem to be oblivious to this discomfort. The passageway becomes wider and taller allowing the two to stand and walk up right. Ben stops to rest.

"How are you holding out," Ben asks as he takes a long drink from his canteen.

Bruce takes off his pack, "I'm doing good, feels good to stand up though. I hope there isn't any more like that. Are you alright?"

"Yes, I'm fine. I don't think there is much chance of us getting lost so far. No other corridors just this one, I don't want to take any chances though, and that is why I brought this chalk along. Every time we venture off this main corridor or rest I will place an, 'X' with an arrow pointing to the exit."

"Good idea," Bruce looks at his watch, "It's nearly nine a.m. do you want something to eat?"

"No, I want to get moving again. The passage looks like it's widening out up ahead. We should cover more ground now." Ben says shining his light ahead of them.

Bruce slings his backpack onto his back following Ben whose pace has rapidly increased. The passageway opens into a large subterranean room. Ben and Bruce marvel at this site as Ben shines his flashlight around the room. Large stalagmites and giant boulders dwarf them. From the ceiling hang large stalactites. Both men stand in awe as the light barely reaches the far side of the chamber.

"What is that over there," Bruce points to a spot near them, "...looks like there's been a fire here."

"Sure does! It must have been a hot one cause there isn't any charcoal or ash," Ben walks over to the spot to get a closer look, "Smells like sulfur," the rocks in the area are covered in a fine white powder, "Yes sir, if I had to guess that's what I would say it is, sulfurs."

"Sulfur, who uses sulfur to make fire, a blacksmith?"

"I don't know. Maybe the Aborigine priests were here and ignited a sulfur deposit?"

"Wouldn't that kill them, and if so where are their bodies."

"Hmm...I don't know Bruce. This is strange though," Ben shines his light around the boulders, "Hey look over there," a shiny object is reflecting the light. Ben quickly walks over to the object and picks it up, "It's a tie clip," Bruce rushes to join him, "look, on the back it has this engraving, 'Senator Newton'."

"I thought you said no one knew about this cave and that the Aborigine didn't come down here because it is holy to them," Bruce asks puzzled.

Ben is now questioning the secrecy of the cave.

"I can't explain this Bruce, and I'm not going to try. There is no way for me to determine how long this clip has been here, or how long ago the fire was here. In these cave's things metallic shouldn't last long with the humidity and all, but then again who knows. We will take this with us, and when we get back we will check on this, Newton."

"Sounds good to me, now let's get some marks on these boulders and find our way through here. This place is giving me the creeps," Bruce says while shining his flashlight around the chamber.

Ben begins marking the boulders with chalk as they walk the entire circumference of the room only to find one other corridor opposite of the one they came in.

"Well, that settles it doesn't it. I guess we have only one choice Bruce and this is it," Bruce nods his approval as Ben shines his light down the passage. A cold draft gently brushes against their faces.

"Burr, how deep are we Ben?"

"I don't know. We've been gradually going down since we started. There must be an opening down there somewhere."

Cautiously, they step into the dark corridor. A freezing breeze blows up the corridor from some place ahead. They sop and put on their jackets as Ben stares at a faint light shining around a distant bend, and as they get closer the light becomes more intense, the air becomes crisper. The corridor turns abruptly up a rock embankment to a darkened sky. They struggle to climb the loose gravel.

Finally reaching the top they behold a sky filled with dark flying figures, and a man dressed in white standing before them. Ben falls to his knees. Bruce stands stunned looking at Michlu.

"Welcome to Nicboth. I've been waiting for you," Michlu approaches them and Bruce backs away slowly, "Don't be frightened, I mean you no harm," Michlu reaches down touching Ben's head, "Do not kneel before me. I'm an angel here to protect you while you do your work." Ben slowly raises his head and stands. Bruce looks at Ben who is smiling, and then at Michlu. Bruce's first instinct is to run back into the cave, but he is too afraid to move.

"N...now wait a minute. You're an angle," Bruce points a shaky finger toward Michlu.

"Yes, my name is Michlu, and yours is Bruce, his is Ben."

"How did you know that," Bruce pauses for a moment to think and then walks towards Michlu with his hand extended in a rush, "Ok, I get it. You're an old friend of Ben's right, and this place is an old hang out of yours that Ben knew about," Bruce stops his rush next to Ben, and stands facing Michlu.

"No, not exactly," Michlu speaks softly, "Ben is an old friend of mine, but I have never shown myself to him until now. This place is called, Nicboth, it is a resting place. Normally, no man is allowed here. We do make acceptation's, with his dad, and now with you two."

"Sure," Bruce is still not convinced, "and where are all these other angels?"

"Bruce, you have so little faith. I understand your skepticism, so please step out here with me," Michlu reaches out and touches Bruce on the shoulder. Something stirs inside Bruce the moment

Michlu touches him. Bruce looks into Michlu's blue eyes and feels he can trust him.

"Ah, well, sure," as Bruce steps out from behind the rocks all the angels stand and look at him.

Bruce looks in amazement at the large group of angels whose abundance stretches all around the mountain as far as he can see. All around him are angels dressed in traditional white ropes, and tied around their waist is a gold rope. Radiance shines from their very essence as if they were made of gold or the finest silver. He drops to his knees and begins to pray.

Michlu kneels next to him, "Its ok. We will not harm you," Michlu then turns to Ben, "Come and join us."

"Yes, I will do just that," Ben smiles and walks to Bruce's side and kneels next to him, "Hey, are you alright," he asks softly.

"Yes, well maybe…is this real? I mean…I'm not dreaming…right," Bruce's eyes fill with tears, and Ben hugs Bruce.

"Bruce…it is all real, really," Ben helps Bruce to his feet, "These are all real angels

The angels throw their fist into the air, cheering loudly startling Bel.

* * *

"De, what is your report! The sounds coming from the mountain sound like war," Bel growls.

"I sent Wit to watch Michlu as you ordered and he approaches now," De points toward the sky above the rocks. Wit's flight is furious and reckless as he zooms to Bel. At one point his altitude is to low and the tip of one-wing turns to ash as it dips into the invisible boundary causing him to spin out of control. He lands with a thud at Bel's feet.

"Report," Bel demands.

Wit pushes himself upright, and then stands, "There is a cave in that outcrop, and two humans are now on Nicboth."

"What, impossible! I wonder what kind of trick Michlu is playing," Bel jumps onto a large boulder and looks toward the crowd of angels gathered around the outcrop. Word spreads through out the demon ranks about the humans.

They gather around Bel and swarm once again in the skies above Nicboth.

CHAPTER 8
The Joining

Cold wind spins snow in a corner of an alley lifting it, tossing it to the side with a sudden gust. Paper hangs from a trash bin fluttering in the wind. It would take flight if it were not for the trash holding it in place.

The alley stretches from the mid-section of, Stevens Blvd, to the corner of West Elm and Chestnut. On the north side of the alley is an old shoe plant, long since abandon, with its old crumbling red brick, and broken windows.

To the south side of the alley is a seven-foot old stonewall running the alleys entire length. Just on the opposite side of the wall is an eight-foot chain-link fence, with angled barbwire projecting over the top of the wall giving onlookers the impression of a prison.

The barrier surrounds the, "Murphy and Son," warehouse. It, like the shoe plant, is abandon. Weathered brown grasses poke through the asphalt cracks of the parking lot, and stand tall on what was a lush lawn decades ago. The weeds sway in the breeze along the fence and throughout the warehouse grounds.

An iron gate remains the only strong fixture remaining on the grounds. It stands between two large columns of stone preventing entrance onto the premises. The crumbly, gray black top drive leads to the main entrance then to a large parking lot where brown weeds grow rampant in its cracks. Lining the drive, centered in the parking lot is tall lamppost, mounted on cracked concrete piers. The lamppost with their lights long since broken out, stand tall and firm as sentries in the abandon grounds. Sitting on top of one of the lights is, Danatallion.

Danatallion is a Duke of Hell—very powerful with thirty-six legions of demons under his command. He is gifted in the arts and sciences, with the ability to know the thoughts of most people— he can change most of these thoughts to his will. He can also cast the impression of love and imitate the likeness of any person; he can show visions, and cause a person to imagine anything he wills.

Artists usually depict him as a man with many appearances, which means the faces of any man or women. There are also depictions in which he holds a book in one of his hands. In a fifth-tenth century painting he is dressed in blue and holds a Bible. In a drawing dated to the early renaissance he stands as a woman, holding the globe in one hand and a Bible in the other. Still, in modern times as an early American pioneer—a statue in a park holding a book of Scientology.

Today he is not in disguise and sits on his perch looking toward the western skies. He watches for two legions of demons to join him.

His patience wears thin; waiting was never one of his traits. He wants this over so he can move on. He sits on his lofty perch picking his gnarly teeth with a sharp piece of bone, while gripping his claws tightly around the light cap; stretching his wings every now and then to relief the amenity of this prolonged wait; his eyes glow red and fade to ruby embers, pulsating with the rage building within him. Smoke rolls from his nostrils as flame begin to glow yellow inside the cavity. His jet black body begins to quake as he can no longer hold back the consuming anger of contorted apparitions flooding his psyche.

He will discipline the worms when they arrive.

In the distance a dark blot moves toward him growing larger as it does. The blot moves closer it takes on more detail. The demon wings stroke the air sending wafts of sounds cascading to Danatallions pointed ears. His legions are approaching.

Smika is the first to land circling Danatallion before landing at the base of the lamp.

Danatallion glares down at her unfurling his large wings. He stands on top of the light pole with red fiery eyes glowing down on Smika.

Smika tucks her tail between her legs looking down at the pavement.

She squeaks softly, "We were late because a great army of angels patrol the Heavens near Nicboth...w...we could not get past them, but for fear of being late went around rather than fighting our way through them."

Danatallions eyes grow cooler turning pink. He furls his wings before leaping from the pole to the lot next to Smika, who cowers into a fetal position covering her head with her wings. Danatallion does not speak, but pats Smika before walking off watching the rest of his legions land.

"We will take rest here and wait for Bel before we begin... You did give Bel the message," Danatallion asks as he watches his legion s land all around them.

"No, I...I could not, forgive me, but the angels were thick moving in large numbers to Nicboth...I...I would have need to fight them all to carry out your orders," Smika cowers closer to the light pole looking with one eye quizzically toward Danatallion who is standing with his back toward her. She has more information and feels she must tell him before he looses patience with her. She shouts with a raspy voice, "They are led by A'albiel."

Danatallion lowers his sight to the ground as Smika's words enter his ears. He spins around and steps to Smika and then squats next to her. His voice is soft...almost a whisper, "A'albiel works along side Michelle. If A'albiel is leading the charge to Nicboth then Michelle must be lurking about somewhere with his legions...looking for us."

Danatallion pats Smika on her wings before he raises his hands above his head, "Listen to me," His voice thunders quieting the mob of fiends which fill the entire grounds; sitting perched on the top of the stonewall, and roof of the warehouse or watch with glowing yellow eyes from the shadows beyond the broken glass inside the warehouse. Danatallion looks all around at the two legions of small demons. He chose these especially as he has need for stealth and cunning.

"Of all my legions I chose you for this purpose. I know you will not fail me..., but we should listen to the wind and hear its call... Michelle is sending A'albiel to Nicboth to free his angels from Bel, while he looks for me and I'm sure he is, for the last time we met at the flood he swore to watch after me and his duty is to keep me at bay. So, listen, listen clearly—time is of the core. Move swiftly to your assignments and take charge of your trust as not to let them flee. Once you have them, hold them until the hour of the twelfth moon. Then strike your charges as to kill them. Not before nor after, but on the hour strike, and slay your trust," as he speaks he walks slowly across the pavement toward the wall. Looking up to the Heavens he sees a white dot in the distance—Michelle has found him, "Take flight now and GO! Do your work in haste and then wait for the hour!"

As he speaks the devilish sprits leap into the air unfurling their wings, clacking like a flock of birds screeching into the night. They fly off in various directions.

Danatallion looks up at the white dot which is now closer, "...and we will see if you can catch me," Danatallion leaps into the air and disappears.

Smika lowers her wing, peeks out above it, and finds she is all alone. Above her she hears the wafting of wings and a bright blinding light shines down on her.

She raises her wing covering her eyes.

* * *

"Lord, have mercy on me! I swear I never saw anything like this in all my days," Thelma gasps as she looks out the third story window of Charlotte's room.

The snow covers many of the cars in the parking lot. With very few exceptions most businesses closed early allowing their employees to leave before the main brunt of the storm hit. Even with the warning, the speed of the blizzard trapped many on the interstates before they had a chance to escape.

Hospitals and emergency shelters are open in many large communities where full time staff keeps them going, but in the rural areas most shelters are closed. Small emergency centers run by the sheriff departments, or the EMC maintain communications by radio or cell phone with those outside the reach of natures cold embrace. Travel by ground vehicles is impossible, and air flight is hazardous to say the least. Some pilots on duty at local hospitals, police stations, state highway patrols, large government complexes, and news stations, took the initiative and started their helicopters blowing the snow off the heliports. Many did not, and find themselves ensnared by the world of snow and ice.

Wentzville hospital was lucky to have on staff a full time pilot and he had the foresight to start his bird once an hour to keep the pad clear. The hospital custodians kept the pathway from the hospitals rear entrance to the pad shoveled creating a canyon made of snow to the helicopter.

Thelma steps back from the window rubbing her bare arms. Like many people, she is dressed for the heat not for this, the snow and cold. Her shift ended hours ago, but where is she to go? The snowdrifts block most exits, and those that are clear lead to deep snow, besides something inside her churns, telling her to stay and not to worry about the weather. She turns to Charlotte who sleeps soundly, and picks up the clipboard hanging on a hook at the foot of the bed.

The charts indicate Charlotte is doing well. The medication is doing its job—she will recover.

Thelma places the clipboard back on its hook, steps out of the room, and turns down the hall to the nurse's station.

Outside the window lurks Ce. He steps through the brick and mortar wall easily into Charlotte's room where he stands at the foot of her bed. He stands upright while raising his hands outstretched over the bed.

"Du-may tid-da alba su-tay… Du-may tid-da alba su-tay… Du-may tid-da alba su-tay," Ce chants then steps around to the head of the bed.

The room fills with a green smoke and thickens as Ce chants, "Du-may tid-da alba su-tay."

Thelma, burst into the room with a long metal pole swinging it at Ce.

Ce jumps back hissing at her.

"Don't you hiss at me you rigidity old devil, you…now scat," Thelma swings the pole at Ce again.

Ce ducks, growling at Thelma while reaching out with his sharp claws, but Thelma strike's him with the pole.

"In the name of Jesus, (Ce covers his ears) leave this woman alone! You have no power here, your spells contain nothing, but your foul order…Now Get," Thelma demands.

Ce steps away from Thelma still covering his ears and wails, "What are you doing here?"

"I should be asking you the same thing, but since I already know I won't! I said be gone from this place…The Lord protects her," Thelma swings the metal pole almost striking Ce.

Ce leaps from the room, through the wall and into the storm where he disappears into the night.

Thelma turns back to Charlotte. She pretends to wipe the dirt from her uniform, "And still champ… Thelma."

Charlotte opens her eyes and sees Thelma dressed as an angel in a pure white robe with a gold rope tied around her waist.

Thelma walks over to Charlotte's side, places her hand on her forehead and looks deep into her green Irish eyes. She says softly, "How ya doing kid," then she smiles.

Charlotte looks up at her, and says weakly, "Thank you," before giving Thelma a quick smile and then closes her eyes.

Thelma closes her eyes, "Lord you have a fine servant in Charlotte, may you continue protecting her and keeping her in your well of love," Thelma smiles at Charlotte, "Praise the Lord!"

* * *

Newton sits confidently staring out the window of, Air Force One, while slowly rubbing his chin. His thoughts focus on the meeting with the President and the assignment he is now undertaking. He opens the briefcase on his lap pulling out five thin manila file folders. He opens one after the other retrieving the 8 x 10 photographs out of each one, before placing the folders back into the briefcase snapping the lid closed. He lays the photographs on top of the briefcase and stairs at the first one.

The stewardess serves him his drink while smiling brightly at him briefly interrupting his concentration. Without thanking her he returns to the photos.

The President rests peacefully in his makeshift office aboard the plane, while watching a rerun of the Ohio State Michigan football game played several weekends ago—with his schedule he must take in enjoyment when he can. The meeting with Que and Newton did not bother him, but the assignment Que sent them on turns his stomach. To take his mind off it he watches the game...so far it is working to relax him.

About two hundred yards off each wing tip is an F-18 escorting Air Force One. One of the F-18 pilots watches a strange sight. He watches a dark mass—like a flock of birds—move parallel with them, but thousands of feet lower. This mass does not appear on his radar screen.

"Ah, Six-Seven Zulu, do you copy, over."

"This is Six-Seven Zulu, we copy Red Leader, over."

"Six Seven Zulu do you read anything below us about three-thou, over"

"That's a negative Red leader, over."

"How about visual, do you see a flock of birds below us, over."

"That's affirmative, commander, is something jamming....what is that," Six-Seven Zulu banks hard right then banks hard left to avoid two dark projectiles.

"Red Leader, Red leader this is...." Six Seven Zulu looks to his right in time to see Red leader explode. Pieces of Red Leaders plane burst from the red and yellow ball of swirling flame in all directions. The explosion rocks Air Force One, but those on board give the shaking to nothing more than a turbulent.

Air Force One's pilots find it disturbing. They monitor all

broadcast and on their radar screen Red Leaders indicator disappears.

"Red Leader, Red Leader, this is Red Dawn, come in, over."

Silence

"Six Seven Zulu do you copy, over"
"Yes, this is Six-Seven Zulu; I copy you Red Dawn, over."
"Do you have visual on Red leader, over?"
"That is a negative Red Dawn, Red Leader was repor...."
Six—Seven Zulu's broadcast is suddenly cut short....Air Force ones pilots call out desperately, "Six-Seven Zulu, Six-Seven Zulu do you copy...do you copy..."

Silence

If they could see behind them they would see another red and yellow mass of swirling flames from Six-Seven Zulu's plane as it explodes.

The two pilots look at each other then scramble emergency procedures, but as they flip the levers to change radio frequencies and engage the planes hidden weaponry they find the switches are all dead.

Checking their maps they find they are nearing their final destination—St. Louis International Airport.

Surrounding the plane is the dark mass from below—a dark mass of demons.

* * *

"Are you sure the driveway is this way," Sharon shouts to Sam as she throws another shovel full of snow. The snow in Defiance is nearly eight feet deep. Sam is doing the best he can to guide their efforts to the road.

"Yes, I believe so, I'm following the rock of the driveway. We have about another twenty feet to go and then we should reach the road. I heard the snow plows earlier so the roads may be clear," Sam shouts back. He is ahead of Sharon, who is by the house scrapping loose snow from the five-foot wide path.

Charles carries in firewood from the shed. Sam first dug a path there before digging toward the road and Charles wants to be useful and carries in armloads of wood for the fire.

Snow falls lightly as Charles pauses to catch his breath. He watches the snow as it floats down to the ground. He cannot see much beyond the top of the snow, but he can hear birds chirping some distance away. The sun peeks through briefly sending a glimmer of sunlight reflecting off the metal of a plane as it banks for it s final approach into Lambert International Airport. Charles squints trying to see the plane clearly through his aged eyes.

"Sam! Sharon! Look at the plane," Charles shouts as he recognizes the insignia.

"Air Force One…my, oh my, I wonder what its doing," Sharon says as she leans her shovel against the snow wall, "I'm surprised the airport is open."

"Probably a headline trip, 'President fly's over snow ravaged area,' that sort of thing," Sam says as he throws a shovel of snow without hardily a glance at the plane, "One thing I know for sure he won't help us dig out of here."

"Yeah, suppose you're right about that…nice lookin' plane though," Charles mutters as he rest against the shed door watching the plane slowly turn toward its approach.

"You know, for some reason I have a bad feeling about all

this," Sharon pushes her shovel through the loose snow tossing a scope over the top of embankment.

* * *

Two small angels, Thomas and Angela, sit on top of the embankment watching the plane then look knowingly at each other for they share Sharon's intuition. They can see the demons swarming around the plane and the large darkened clouds rushing over the horizon to join their demonic brethren.

Angela prays while Thomas stands raising an open palm above his head toward the dark mass, "You will be concurred," he states somberly then leaps off the embankment landing next to Sam. He looks up at Angela.

She raises her head from prayer, looks down at Thomas, then nods while a tear runs down her cheek.

Thomas returns the nod looking toward the expanse of sky above him, "May your will be done Lord," Thomas darts into the sky above Sam about two hundred feet before turning toward earth with his teeth clinched, his arms outstretched in front of him, and with his fist squeezed tightly together he plunges through the snow into the earth next to Sam.

Sam tosses another shovel full of snow as he suddenly feels the earth beneath his feet shake.

He pauses wondering if what he felt was real or was it his old legs tiring beneath him. The ground shakes again then quakes causing Sam to lose his footing and fall to the ground.

The snow walls on either side of Sam collapse on top of him.

Sharon steps inside the house just as a large mass of snow slides off the roof.

Charles falls to the ground crawling across the shacking path to the shed as the snow walls around him fall.

* * *

Air Force One lands at Lambert International Airport rounding the far runway as it taxis toward the terminal.

Newton watches the snow plows on an adjacent runway shooting tall flumes of snow into the air as they clear another landing strip. He snaps the lid of his briefcase shut then continues staring out the window.

A stewardess walks down the center aisle checking passengers asking if there is anything she can do for them, "Senator is there anything I can do for you?"

Newton turns from the window toward the sweet voice looking directly into the eyes of Ce'. The demons hairy snout and thin eyes push in on him. Newton pushes himself away pressing himself against the window, covering his head.

"Senator, Senator," the stewardess yells as she backs away.

Newton slowly lowers his arms peeking out to find the stewardess and an older man leaning over him.

"Are you ok," the stewardess asked while rubbing Newton's shoulder.

The Senator doesn't say a word. He slides down into his seat, very shaken. He looks up at the older man who is walking away shaking his head and muttering, "Drunk…pathetic!"

Newton nervously looks up at the stewardess who is rubbing his shoulder. She smiles at him then for a brief, moment Ce face overlays the stewardesses. The Senator begins to push away, but the image fades. Newton looks around anxiously for fear of Ce crawling from under the seat or climbing through the window.

"Senator, are you alright?"

"Yes, yes…me…I think so," Newton says as he looks around.

"I didn't mean to frighten you. You must've been sleeping and…."

"No that's alright…really…I'm…ah, just fine," Newton says trying his best to reassure the stewardess.

"Ok then," the stewardess smiles at Newton going to the next set of passengers.

The senator wonders how much more of this he can take before he snaps….then he remembers the words of Bel, "…*we choose you senator for a calling greater than any other!*"

As he begins to relax the plane shakes violently.

The luggage compartments pop open casting their contents in the aisle; passengers bounce around in their seats; oxygen mask drop down and bounce on their rubber cords; the stewardess falls down in the aisle while a loud alarm beeps.

Newton turns looking out the window in time to see a large crack, five feet wide, race down the runway. In the distance he can hear explosions. Dark clouds of smoke swirl from beyond a distant stand of trees.

Air Force one slows abruptly adding to the shaking. Its engines roar as the pilot turns the plane toward the terminal then stops with a sudden jolt as it arrives at its gate.

The crack races down the runway as the earth on either side of it lunges upward and then down. A deafening roar rumbles as it moves with increasing speed. Buildings sway and some topple. The St. Louis Arch breaks in half at it s greatest height as the crack rips and tears the earth between its legs. The giant structure falls in opposite directions; its north leg falls into the Mississippi river while its south leg falls into the city and across Interstate Seventy—narrowly missing tall buildings. Water from the river pours into the abyss. Steam rises from deep within its core.

Outside the city the crack blisters down the river to New

Madrid, Missouri. The site of the eighteen-eleven earthquake that changed the course of the Mississippi River while ringing church bells as far away as Philadelphia, Penn. As the crack moves south it sinks deep into the marrow of the earth. Like a shark preparing to strike it dives deep and the earth becomes still—tranquil.

People pick themselves up and stare at the desolation before them. Snow and ice line the banks of the churning river as steam rises from the void. Steam rolls into the frigid air and the wind blows it back into the city where it freezes on trees, buildings, roads...anything it touches.

At the airport, the Presidential Helicopter is taking off. Newton sits across the aisle from the President who sits relaxed reading some papers handed to him by an aide. The Senator turns to look out the helicopter window near him and beholds a squadron of demons flying in formation along side the helicopter. He sits back in his seat not wanting to believe his eyes. He looks again, and the flying demons are waving at him....smiling. Newton slowly sits back into his seat looking across the aisle at the President. To his amazement he sees a demon sitting next to the President and two more sitting in the seats before and behind him. The President sits nonchalantly reading then he looks toward Newton, "Why are you surprised," the President, says, "...they follow me wherever I go."

* * *

White....A sheet of white blocks the doorway in front of Sharon as she stands rubbing her hands trying to bring warmth to numb fingers. She fell back into the kitchen, knocked off her feet as the ground shook beneath her. She pushed herself back from the avalanche as it piled relentlessly in the doorway then she tried desperately to dig out. Her efforts were in vain as the cold got the best of her. She now looks around for her gloves.

Sam opens his eyes to grayish white before him. He feels the weight of the snow on him which pins his legs and arms to an icy tomb. He struggles to move his legs, but the weight is more than he can move.

Charles stands in the shed doorway looking at an impossible wall of snow. The shed entrance he cleared earlier to provide a wide path for the three of them. Charles can see the red tiles of the roof, but any familiarity with the path Sam dug is completely gone. The walls of the snowy canyon collapsed leaving mounds of snow. Why the entrance of the shed was spared Charles figures is luck. The brunt of the snow fell off the roof burying the kitchen doorway compounded by the walls of the canyon collapsing around it. Charles wonders about Sam and Sharon…wondering if they are alive. Something inside him begins to stir.

"Sam…Sharon," Charles calls.

Silence, only the wind and the distant chirp of a bird.

After several calls he turns to the shed where he finds a snow shovel.

Sharon Steps back from the frozen entrance into the living room where the fireplace yields little relief as the fire is out with only small red coals glowing from the hearth. Most light is blocked by the snow covering the windows. Some light penetrates through casting a white dull glow. Sharon stumbles toward the fireplace trying to see. Her breath fogs in the air around her as she pulls her hands inside her coat sleeves.

"Where did those gloves go…I was wearing them and they just disappeared," she hears a thud at her feet. By her feet lay her gloves, "How in the world," Sharon mutters as she bends down picking them up.

"I'll tell you how," whispers a voice from the shadows in the corner behind her.

Sharon stops as she hears the whisper then slowly turns around. At first she thought the voice familiar, maybe Sam or Charles. Their voice shallow from exhaustion after digging through the snow then her eyes adjust to the dim light. In the shadows she sees a faint dark figure rocking back and fourth on its hind legs.

The creature steps out from its shadowy confines into the dim light. The lips of its long snout turned up bearing its teeth.

"A wolf," Sharon mutters as she steps backward.

Sam pushes against the snow at his back, compacting the snow above him. Somewhere he read about survivors of avalanches doing this creating a small pocket where their body heat would keep them warm…although Sam does not believe it as his hands and toes grow colder by the second. He hears the sound of Charles snow shovel.

"Hey…under here…HEY," Sam shouts.

Charles hears something muffled and pauses. A bird flutters past.

"It was only a bird," Charles continues digging.

"Hey….Sharon….Charles….HEY," Sam begins digging toward the scrapping and crunching.

Charles pauses once again looking skyward for another bird when he feels something grab his leg.

"Aaaaaahhhhh," Charles shouts and smacks the attacker with the flat part of the shovel.

"Ouch! What are doing…stop hitting me," Sam tumbles from the mound of snow and lands at Charles's feet. Charles looks down at Sam and Sam up at Charles. They both begin laughing. That's when they hear Sharon scream.

"Sharon…come on let's go," Sam shouts. The two begin

digging the snow from in front of the doorway. Sam pulls the snow from the top of the doorway with his gloved hands. While Charles digs at the base with the shovel.

CHAPTER 9
The Hunt

Night...cold, ice sickles hang from tall trees as snow lightly falls from a gray midnight sky. Charles and Sam finish digging out the driveway to the main road to find a mountain of road slush. Sam stands at the foot of his driveway looking up at the sight. Some twenty feet it seems yet there is no time to lose. Sharon has vanished from the house.

Charles sits down in the snow next to Sam exhausted from his work, "What...now," Charles asks forcing the words out between each labored breath while looking up at the mountain of snow before him.

"I guess we climb...or I will anyway," Sam suggests while looking down at Charles, "Are you ok?"

"Sure...I mean, I will be as soon as I rest...You go ahead. I will go on back to the house," Charles doesn't look up at Sam, but speaks while looking down at the snow at Sam's feet, "Go ahead, really I'm alright."

Sam kneels next to Charles placing his hand on his shoulder, "Charlie old buddy you're not fooling me. I'll help you back to the house before I leave."

"Sure, thanks Sam. Where are you going anyway?"

"My boss's house is up the road half a mile. He has several farm tractors with scoops I can use to clear this mess from the drive. Charles, in just a few hours we will be on the road to town."

"Yep, if that's the case, let's go," Charles says as he starts to stand. Sam helps him to his feet and they walk to the house.

* * *

Charlotte lays in her bed looking out the window. The hospital is on emergency power. All unnecessary lighting is out leaving patient rooms dimly lit. Although day time the sky is overcast with ever increasing dark clouds. She rolls onto her back looking around the room at the darkened corners. From under her room door a thin beam of light projects across her polished linoleum floor a few feet before the darkness swallows it like a black hole. The light comes from a nurse's station a few feet outside her door across the hall.

She listens to the stillness. At times she can hear the muffled chatter from the nurse's station. Then at times a squeaky wheel of a gurney or cart accompanied by the rattling of something metallic, bed pans she guesses, but most of the time it is quiet, still. She turns her attention toward the window again. She can see the suns haze behind the gray clouds. Snowflakes lightly fall with some landing on her window ledge. Her eyes gaze into the horizon beyond the glass as her mind drifts to Charles. She smiles, remembering how he worried over her.

"Nothing to worry about now dear, I'm fine," she whispers. Her eyes focus on the reflection of the light shining from under the door on the window. Then her thoughts drift again to the nurses. Her infection is in check. The antibiotics are doing their job. Her thoughts are clear, focused. Closing her eyes she says a silent prayer. As she opens them her eyes focus on the reflection in the window where she sees two yellow dots.

She rolls over looking toward the door where Ce is looking back at her.

* * *

Charles sits down at the makeshift research table in Sam's living room. Sam carries an oil lamb in from the kitchen to the table.

"Here ya go Charles. I left the lamb oil and matches in the kitchen. Also, I set up a propane stove on the kitchen table for you to heat up soup you'll find in the pantry. You should have plenty of firewood."

"Thanks Sam. I'll be alright, but I can't help wonderin' what happen to her."

"I don't know Charles, but I bet it has something to do with all this," Sam points to the stack of documents and artifacts.

"Yep," Charles says as his eyes drop to a stack of papers in front of him.

"You'll be ok," Sam asks while pulling on his heavy coat.

"Yep, you won't be gone long, no how. I'll just sit here looking over this stuff," Charles points to the artifacts on the table.

Sam nods then smiles before turning toward the kitchen. As he steps out the back door his breath fogs in front of him. A cold wind chills his face, reddening his cheeks. Clouds push in from the northwest carrying the promise of more snow, blocking the moon. His thoughts remain focused on finding help as he steps away from the house with the snow crunching under foot.

Charles stands at the backdoor watching Sam walk away. He isn't sure if this is a good idea, staying here all alone. Sharon vanishes leaving no clues. What could have happened to her? He and Sam checked the small house several times through finding nothing more than dust bunnies for their efforts. He sits down at the table where he picks up a manila envelope, "Whelp, maybe there's a clue in this mess somewhere."

He begins looking through a stack of papers when he hears a soft scratching and gnawing coming from the woodpile next to the fireplace across the room from him. A mouse is making himself at home, he thinks to himself and continues his search, shuffling some papers then stacking them next to the others.

The mouse scratches louder.

Charles walks across the room to the woodpile where the sound grows two fold.

"Must be a big old mouse to make all that racket," he pulls logs from the stack laying them on the floor behind him. As he pulls one log after the other the scratching becomes louder and faster. The stack is down to the last row of logs resting on the wood rack. Charles kneels looking under the rack and behind it, "Hmmm, no little mousey here."

He stands and slides the rack from the wall. The scratching becomes noticeably louder. Charles stands still listening to the scraping and the gnawing. He kneels once again turning his ear to the floor. The sound...It sounds more like a voice speaking to him.

He lowers himself slowly closer until he is on all fours with his ear inches from the floor.

"We have..." the voice trails off drowned out by the gnawing and scratching. He lowers himself closer placing his ear directly on the floor. He listens, as the scratching grows louder then suddenly stops.

Charles lifts his head in alarm at the sudden stillness wondering if he imagined the voice. Then he hears a faint whisper, almost like a sigh, coming from the floor. He lowers his head to listen.

His eyes grow wide as the voice suddenly becomes distinct, "Charles run!" It is Charlotte's voice.

He lifts his head in bewilderment, "It couldn't be...how? Charlotte, honey." he says in a whisper with his nose an inch above the wood floor.

He hears the sound of footsteps behind him. As Charles turns around he stares into the narrow eyes of Ce.

* * *

Hebrew draws his sword, but Angela stops him, "This is the way it must be for now," She says to him, "The time will come when Ce is all yours."

Hebrew sheaths his sword, "God in the highest knows all. I trust he will deliver Ce into my hands."

* * *

Darkness surrounds Sharon as she feels the rough ground around her. She doesn't understand what happened. One minute she's staring into the eyes of a wolf, then here. Down on her hands and knees she feels ahead as she crawls. Her fingers touch something hairy.

She gasps and scoots backward.

From the dark void ahead of her she hears a soft low growl, followed by the sudden snapping together of sharp teeth inches from her face, then the fowl odor causing her to gag.

"Welcome, welcome to my home away from home," softly Amy growls. Amy is the fifty-eigth spirit, a President of Hell. Demoted after being the seventh sprit for many years. Only Lucifer and two others no the reason why. She seeks to regain her former glorie by helping Que.

Suddenly, from behind Sharon a small fire erupts, she turns toward it. The light cast its illumination all around, but the vastness and expanse of the cave is beyond the lights reach. She can see in the distance, past the lights brilliance, the shimmer of the flame on large stalactites, and stalagmites, sparkling like diamonds.

"I'm in hell," she mutters.

"No, not exactly," Amy says sending Sharon reeling backwards. She looks around, but sees only the darkness beyond the fire light. Behind her she hears footsteps.

In the dimness where light and dark fade into an obscure haze she sees someone walking toward her. It is a woman dressed in hospital clothes. It is Charlotte.

"Charlotte," Sharon shouts then runs to her, holding her close.

Charlotte doesn't speak, but smiles broadly as she hugs Sharon. Then she steps back from Sharon and looks at her, "Do you know where we are?"

"No, and I don't like it," Sharon whispers as she looks around, "We are not alone."

Charlotte looks around then looks into Sharon's eyes, "Who, who is here?"

"I'm not sure," Sharon says nervously.

She holds Charlotte close as they walk toward the fire, when in the darkness they hear rocks clattering together, a vague figure, dark and tall moving toward them.

As the figure moves closer Charlotte's eyes grow wide, "Charles," she hurries her step.

Sharon holds onto Charlotte walking with her to Charles.

"Charlotte, oh I'm glad to see you," Charles hugs Charlotte gently, "Are you alright?"

"Yes, yes, I'm fine, except I'm not sure where we are. Are we dead and this is hell," Charlotte asks while wrapping her arms around Charles.

Charles looks into his wife's eyes, "Now, you don't fret none. I'm sure that Jesus feller is looking out for you."

"Us Charles, us," Charlotte says while looking around.

Sharon moves closer to the fire followed by Charles and Charlotte, "We are not alone in here," Sharon says in almost a whisper.

"Who," Charles asks.

"Me," Amy says gently.

The trio stands silently looking around, but do not see anyone.

From deep within the shadows before them they hear a soft laugh. Soft, almost a hush at first then the laughter grows louder until it becomes a shattering cackle echoing throughout the cave. They stand close together covering their ears, then the laughter abruptly stops.

"Charles…Charles Hanson, you're a striking old devil for someone of your age," Amy's disembodied voice echoes.

"Who are you and what do you want with us," Sharon shouts.

"Oh, a feisty one. You must be Sharon, and the woman next to you must be our guest of honor, Charlotte," Amy says while igniting two more fires around them creating a triangle of flame.

Sharon looks a Charlotte, then remembers what Charles told her about Charlotte and her special gift, "What do you want with Charlotte?"

"We want her to stop all her interference…that's all really," Amy then materializes outside the triangle, her face barely visible beyond the yellow flames looks like a wolf with a long snout. Two small horns project out on either side of her forehead. She stands ten feet tall. Her body is shapely beneath a skintight blue body suit.

Sharon sees Amy and begins to march toward her, but

Charlotte grabs her arm, "No honey wait. I know what she wants me to do," Charlotte steps in front of Sharon looking directly into Amy's eyes, "You want me to stop praying for people. You want their souls."

"Why, that's very perceptive of you, but no. You're on a mission, are you not? A mission that involves seeking saints to help you destroy the kingdom my master has built."

"No, I pray for people, that's all I do. I ask for Gods intervention in their lives. Your quarrel with God is your problem," Charlotte says while looking back at Charles.

Amy strolls through the flame changing her-self to appear as a young woman. She wears a full-length black surout with the hood pulled back onto her shoulders. "Your denial does not surprise me," she raises her hand toward Charles, then curls her fingers into a tight fist. She lowers her eyebrows while gnashing her teeth.

Charles grabs his chest in agony, falling to the ground gasping for air. Charlotte and Sharon run over to him.

"What are you doing, let him go," Sharon shouts.

"I will, once Charlotte confesses," Amy says with a laugh.

* * *

Ben stands next to Bruce on the summit of Nicboth wearing layers of clothes and a thick coat. The temperature is ten degrees below zero. Above them the sky darkens with demons. At the mountains base Bel and his demons stand mocking the angels, taunting them.

Ben feels something stir within him, a warm sensation which grows. Then a whisper wafts past his ear, "Bel."

Ben listens intently, but he only hears the wind howling.

"What's the matter Ben, that lizard finally giving you indigestion," Bruce laughs.

"Shhh, I thought I heard something."
Bruce listens, "What?"
"I heard something say, bell."
"Bell...Like a church bell?"
"No, I don't think so," Ben hears something behind him; he turns to find Michlu standing there.
"Ben, I have a task for you," Michlu stares into Bens eyes.
"Does it have something to do with a bell," Ben asks as his gaze returns to the base of the mountain.
"Not a bell, but a demon called Bel. Bel is a demon general, second to a demon Commander, Que. Like all demons, Bel was once an angel, but not your ordinary angel; he was in training to be a powerful archangel. Like the rest he was fooled into rebellion. Now, he is an enemy of God. He is different than most as he understands his mistake. He wants to come back, but doesn't know how. I've talked to him like many others. He refuses to listen because something is holding him. We want you to try."
"Me! If you and the others have talked to him, what do you suppose I say? All of you walk in the grace of God. You've seen Heaven, and so has he. What is it I'm suppose to say to convince him," Ben pleads.
"You were made in the likeness of God. Do not worry about what you are supposed to say. The Holy Sprit will be with you," Michlu says as he bows his head.
Ben watches Michlu for a brief moment then glances at Bruce who is also praying. Inside of him something stirs. That warm sensation returns. He looks at the base of the mountain where the demons appear as little dots, bouncing around and shouting. He remembers his faith, and then about all the events that lead him here, "There must be a reason, maybe this is it," he thinks to himself.
"Yes, you are right," Michlu answers reading Bens mind. He

looks into Ben's eyes and Ben looks deep into his, "This is why you were called."

Ben nods unsure if he really wants to face a demon, but his faith is strong and begins walking down the mountain toward Bel.

Wit glades to a stop at Bels feet, then bows low to the ground. Without looking up he speaks, "A human approaches Sire," then he looks up at Bel, "...I think he comes down to talk with you."

Bel looks up the mountain at Ben who is some distance away, "What, you must be crazy. He can't see us," Bel barks.

"Oh, but he can see the angels. Why couldn't he see us," Wit asks while stepping back.

"We will see," Bel sneers.

Ben's heart thumps rapidly with every step toward the demons. With every step the details of the demons become clearer. He wasn't scared before, now his hands shake. The demons scurry about as he steps closer. Their tails flip high above them. Some remind Ben of large apes with snouts like wolfs, large wings curled on their back and large horns protrude from their skulls. Others like large lizards with wings walking upright, small horns stand almost unnoticed next to their dog like ears. All of them wear leather belts with a sword dangling in sheaths at their sides.

One though stands out from all the rest. A mammoth creature stands over them as if they were toddlers compared to him. His features are human like, although darker, greener is his complexion. Two small horns protrude from his forehead at the hairline, one above each eye. He wears a red Roman gladiator tunic, with a wide leather belt. Hanging from the belt is an empty leather sheath. He also wears leather wrist guards on each arm. The sword he swings above his head wildly. He wears sandals with the straps wrapped around his strong calves.

As Bel swings the sword he shouts obscenities at Ben. The

other demons join him and soon the mountain swells with the roar of taunts, shouts, and screams.

Ben watches all this stopping his march. He is terrified. He wants to run, he wants to turn and run as fast as he can. His heart beats uncontrollably. Confusion runs wild, as he wants to do the Lords will, but wants to flee. Falling to his knees he begins to pray. As he prays he feels a hand on his shoulder.

"Ben, hey, you ok?"

Ben opens his eyes and then looks behind him. He sees Bruce.

"Bruce! What are you doing here? Don't you know the danger you're in," Ben shouts.

"Danger, danger from what," Bruce asks while looking around.

"From what…You don't see….why did you come down here?"

"Michlu said you might need me and asked me to follow you. Hey, isn't it beautiful here?"

"You don't see any demons?"

"Yeah right…demons, where," Bruce asks as he begins to walk forward stepping across the invisible barrier almost onto Python.

Python swings his deadly claws at Bruce, but they waft right through Bruce's leg. Other demons swing at him with their swords. They also waft right through him without any harm.

"The next thing you're going to tell me is that their all around us and how careful I should be," Bruce walks back to Ben who is still kneeling. Bruce sits down next to him, "Am I right or what?"

"Well," Ben begins while looking at a large demon sheathing his sword, "Yes and no…you see," Bruce interrupts him.

"Ben, I asked you to stop doing that," Bruce stands marching up the mountain to Michlu, "Hey, Michlu, can you put a spell or something on him to make him more decisive."

Ben watches the demons while listening to the sound of Bruce's footsteps fade up the mountain, he stands.

As he approaches the demons they act confused. This human sees them.

Ben stops a few yards in front of Python, "Little one, which one is, Bel?"

"Little one," Python screams then lunges forward with his claws scratching Ben across the face leaving four long red streaks down Ben's cheek.

Ben leaps back, crossing the invisible barrier and to safety. He falls to the ground holding his face. The demons move forward stopping short of the line. Ben lays on the rocky soil looking at blood on his hands.

"Mortal, mortals bleed, mortals die," taunts Python.

Ben doesn't know what to say. His face burns from the scratches, his heartbeats fast. What does God want him to say, what does God want him to do? These thoughts race through his mind as the demons stare down on him. He glances around noticing their advance has stopped. They do not come closer. He cautiously stands.

"Which….which one of you is Bel," He asks hoping for a small demon like Python. He looks at the smaller ones wishfully.

"I am Bel," Bel says as he steps next to the boundary.

Ben's eyes grow wide as Bel stands a few yards away towering over him. He swallows hard, "I've come to talk with you," Ben says nervously.

The demons laugh.

Bel bellows, "Michlu sends you to talk to me," Bel pauses then looks up the mountain at Michlu, "…because he is afraid."

The demons around him shout in agreement mixed with obscenities toward Michlu.

"No," Ben says quickly, "God has sent me," Ben boldly proclaims.

Bels glare up the mountain turns toward Ben who is standing confidently staring up at him. Inside Ben burns a new fire ignited by the knowledge he held all along.

"And God isn't going to send me into battle without first equipping me with his armor and his strength!"

"What do you know," Bel sternly says while glaring into Bens eyes.

"I wasn't there when God made all his creations. I wasn't there during the rebellion when he cast you to earth. I only know what the Holy Sprit tells me. Bel, if you want to come back to God he is waiting," Ben says then begins to pray.

All the demons around Nicboth laugh. Bel stares at Ben, "Michlu told you these things," Bel bellows.

"Michlu told me about you. The words come from somewhere else. I know nothing more of you."

"Then why should I speak to you, by what authority do you have here?"

"Let me tell you this, you are lucky to have seen Heaven, to have walked on shining gold Heavenly pavement, and most of all to be once in the presence of God, the maker of all things."

"He's a fraud," Bel barks, and the demons around him shout, "Liar, Fake!"

"Why, why do you call the maker of the all things, including you, a fake," Ben asks sternly. Deep inside an anger stirs.

"Well, Lucifer said..." Bel begins, but Ben interrupts.

"Lucifer is the liar, he is the fake. He is the maker of all lies. What makes you think he is truthful? What makes you think he knows more than God? Was he around in the beginning? Was he there when God spoke and the galaxy was born? Satan, Lucifer was made by God as an archangel, the same as you. Lucifer thought he knew better than God and caused you and many others to revolt. You Bel...You saw his creations. You saw that God initiates all things not for himself, but for his creations."

Bel and rest of the demons within hearing distance listen to every word. They remember the times before, when peace existed in the Heavens before the rebellion.

Ben continues, "Let me ask you this, can a rock move on its own? Can a bird just suddenly exist? Can you make me a demon right now? No, to all these things. In order for a rock to move it must be moved by something. A bird must be created, and its life-force given to it. You or Lucifer cannot create anything from nothing. You must work with what you already have. God creates from nothing at all! Who are you, after seeing, fails to see the truth...A fool that's who!"

Ben turns and walks a few paces away then turns toward Bel who is motionless considering all Ben has said. The rest of the demons murmur, shuffle about, and shout, "Liar, you're the fool," and many obscenities toward Ben.

"Quite," Bel shouts, "He is right...we are the fools," the demons back away from Bel. "Lucifer tricked us. We followed him with no proof, no legitimate reason. God is supreme," Bel lowers his head and prays.

"What are you saying Bel," Python squeaks not believing his pointed ears, "You're not agreeing with him...you can't," he hesitantly uncoils his claws.

In the sky above the demons screech in disbelief, all around Nicboth demons turn toward Bel in anger. They can see his essence is changing. His horns lower into his skull, his skin color changes to a mid-tone caucasian with an olive tint.

Ben reaches over the boundary taking hold of Bel's hand, pulling him toward the boundary.

Bel hesitates.

"It's alright, come on," Ben says tugging on Bel's hand.

Bel closes his eyes and steps over the boundary.

High above the cursing demons of Nicboth glades Danatallion. He slowly swirls, lowering until he is just above the invisible boundary in the sky hovering over Bel.

Bel looks up at him and growls.

Danatallion cackles before landing in the midst of the other demons where he crotches staring at Bel, "So, you've converted. Que thought you might," he lifts his mighty wings high above his head while standing upright. He towers over Bel miniaturizing the tallest demons surrounding him. He flaps his wings vigorously sending rocks, sand and dirt at Ben and Bel.

Ben covers his head with his arms turning away from the onslaught.

Bel watches small stones bounce off Ben then shields him with his wings, covering Ben completely.

* * *

"Hey, thanks for the lift!" Sam says as he waves while standing on the side of the road watching the four-wheel drive pull away. He turns and walks the short distance from the road to the Sheriffs office. The Sheriffs office is located in a rural area just north of Defiance at a wide intersection of two major two-lane roads, N and O. Sam's boss was not at home with the barns locked tight. He needs help to find Sharon.

A swarm of activity greets him as he steps through the doorway. The door pulls a string ringing a bell hanging above the door. No one notices the bell as they hurry by him, carrying boxes, shuffling papers as they rush to a desk or stand discussing the latest storm forecast.

A police scanners lights cycle from left to right as it searches for activity, the stream momentarily stops as an officer's voice hums out of a speaker on the wall, "Officer three-eleven requesting a ten-thirteen," the lights resume their cycle.

Nearby another officer pauses her frantic pace to reply, "Officer three-eleven your ten-thirteen is low twenty-four degrees tonight, two to four inches of snow expected. Strong winds, blowing snow…take your pick, it's just more of the same stuff."

In front of the radio sits the desk clerk shuffling papers. Sam walks over to him.

"Excuse me, can you help me," Sam asks while side stepping a rolling cart, hurriedly pushed by a small heavyset officer.

"Coming through," the officer says to Sam before running the cart down a narrow hallway.

Sam turns back to the clerk. "Can you help me, someone is lost, and I, well…."

The clerk looks up at Sam handing him a stack of papers then says in a low monotone voice, "Fill these out over there on the bench. Take them to Officer Wells when you're through," then he returns to his paper work.

"I really don't think paperwork is going to help me," Sam says sternly.

The clerk looks up at Sam, "Look, we have approximately six officers on duty to cover the entire county. The snow has closed all, but two major interchanges and most of the county is calling us for help. On top of all this the President of the United States is coming here to take our only working four-wheel drive for a joy ride through the disaster zone….Let me asks you this, is the missing person a child?"

Sam shakes his head no.

"Elderly?"

"No."

"Sick, lame, handicapped in anyway?"

"No…not at all. She is a young lady that vanished from my house after the earthquake."

"Vanished?"

"Well she fell back into the house and a bunch of snow slide off the house blocking the doorway. By the time we dug the entrance clean she was gone."

"Gone, vanished…you looked everywhere?"

"Yes."

"Look Mack, I would love to help…." the clerk is interrupted by a flurry of activity at the main doorway. "Excuse me," he says to Sam, but before he can get out of his chair one of the officers rushes over to him.

"It's the President," the young officer says excitedly.

Outside, at the main intersection, a helicopter whirls casting a thick cloud of snow into the air. Sam watches from a window in the one of the sheriffs offices. The clerk stands next to him.

"A road crew spent most of the night clearing that intersection. Now look at it." The clerk says sarcastically before turning toward his desk.

Sam begins to follow the clerk then feels a strong urge to look out the window again. He sees in the swirling snow the outline of several dog-like figures walking around the helicopter. He rubs his eyes and then looks again. The figures are gone. He contributes the sightings to his lack of sleep and hunger.

The blowing snow settles as the Presidential helicopter blades slow to a stop. Three men run from the helicopter to the Sheriffs office. Sam hears the bell above the door ring followed by the clerk greeting the Secret Service agents. He steps out of the office into the hallway listening to the agents speak. Sam doesn't know why, but to him the agents seem fake, almost artificial.

The agents inform the clerk that they are the advance team to make sure the President is safe. The real Presidential Helicopter will be here shortly. They are professional about their task, checking out every room and then frisking and searching everyone in the building including Sam. After their search they hold a quick meeting at the main door. Two go out the front door letting in a cold blast of air. The remaining agent walks over to the clerk and Sam.

"I apologize for the rude entrance and the quick searches, but to us, all that matters is the President and his safety," Agent Bill Adams says as he rubs his hands together.

"Coffee," asks the clerk.'

"Yes, please," Agent Adams turns toward Sam, "Hi, my name is Agent Bill Adams."

Sam and Bill shake hands.

As their hands touch, Sam's mind fills with flying demons, dipping and diving at two figures on a mountain. Looking into the eyes of the agent he sees a snout and sharp teeth project from the agents face. The agent's eyes glow red like hot cinders.

The agent sees Hebrew and Angelina standing next to Sam. He quickly lets go of Sam's hand. The angels disappear from the agent's site, as does the demonic features on the agents face.

Sam steps back in disbelief.

Hebrew whispers in Sam's ear, "Do not worry, we are here with you."

"We," Sam's says aloud.

"Yes, angels sent by God," Angelina whispers.

Sam looks around, but there is no one there. He has a sudden calmness fall over him. Like dew on a spring morning it covers him completely.

Agent Adams stares at Sam. He isn't sure what Sam saw, if anything. He does know in some cases when the curtain of division between good and evil is pierced, mask fall…hidden things emerge…light reveals the darkness.

He raises his radio to call for backup when another agent suddenly appears though the doorway, "The Presidents chopper is landing," he announces.

Agent Adams stares at Sam, "Are you from around here," he asks harshly.

Sam looks into the agents eyes. The red cinders are gone; the snout is just a nose, "Yes, lived around this county most of my life," Sam answers calmly.

"Good, we need a guide. The Sheriff doesn't have anyone to spare," Agent Adams says as he steps through the doorway, then turns back toward Sam, "Well, come on."

Sam stares at the agent wondering if he should go when Hebrew whispers in his ear again, "Go, we will be with you. Don't worry about Sharon."

Sam timidly steps forward then says with a smile, "Let's go."

CHAPTER 10
Charles

Snow swirls on Nicboth. At the entrance of the cave at the outcrop of rocks halfway up the mountain, Bruce and Ben watch Michlu and Bel from a distance.

"Who's that," Bruce asks.

"That is an ex-demon general named Bel," Ben says while packing his backpack.

"Yeah right, seriously...who is that Roman guy? No wait...Norwitch...Norwick, that's it!"

"No Bruce, Norwick is imprisoned in an everlasting storm. That is Bel, a demon general that just accepted Christ. He is no longer demonic, but angelic."

"Ok...whatever, I'm still having a hard time with all this, angels and demon stuff."

"Bruce you see, but still don't believe?" Ben says then lifts the backpack sliding his arm through the shoulder strap.

Bruce helps Ben with the straps, "Oh, I believe, I'm just having a hard time accepting what I see."

"Then you really don't believe. What is it you don't

believe, the demons flying over head or the angels walking around us?"

Bruce smiles at Ben, "Both!"

Ben smiles, "Oh you, come on lets get going."

Ben and Bruce walk over to Michlu and Bel.

"Well, it's time we return to our world. Thank you," Bruce says as he reaches out to shake Bel's hand.

Bel steps back, pulling his sword from its sheath, raising it above his head, "Die you scum," Bel shouts as he swings the blade toward Bruce.

Ben dives at Bruce knocking him to the ground.

Michlu draws his sword piercing a small low flying demon through its chest. Green smoke explodes from the demons nostrils and mouth. He looks down at Ben and Bruce, "To the cave, we are under attack. Go, God is with you," he then swings his sword to the side striking another demon.

Ben and Bruce look on the ground next to them at a large head of a demon with green smoke rolling from its neck. Bruce follows a trail of green blood to the demons hoofs. He looks up at the body still standing on trembling legs; thick, green smoke bellows from its neckline skyward. Bel's sword points to the ground after his follow through. His eyes stare sternly into Bruce's, "Go, now," his voice thunders.

Bruce swallows hard, "Thank you," he says hurriedly as Ben tugs franticly on his shirtsleeve.

"Come on, come on," Ben shouts. The two run toward the cave as demons dive toward them. Angels attack the demons mercilessly, striking the fiends to the ground where they explode in clouds of green smoke, "Hurry," Ben shouts.

Bruce follows close behind Ben, but is in awe of the many demons and angels diving, dipping, dodging and all swinging swords which when struck together send sparks showering through the air. The demons cackle as the angels send praises to God for his strength. Puffs of green smoke rise to the Heavens.

As Ben reaches the cave entrance he looks back for Bruce who is running toward him clumsily stumbling over boulders.

"Come on Bruce, lets go," Ben shouts.

Overhead a large demon dives toward them, but an angel darts between striking the demon across its side. Bruce looses his balance watching this, falling to the ground at Ben's feet. Ben helps him stand, then down the steep slope into the cave, unlatching their flashlight as they run into the narrow tunnel shining the flashlights ahead of them.

Behind them the cackles, clanging swords and yells fade.

Before them, their flashlights shine illuminating the tunnels walls as they rush forward.

Ben grows tired and stops to rest.

"I'm sure we are going in the right direction Bruce."

Bruce does not respond.

Ben looks behind him, but does not see Bruce. He does see something glowing in the darkness causing him to stare, frozen by freight. He sees two thin slights of yellow glowing in the blackness growing wider as they approach. He raises his flashlight just as Ce leaps onto him.

* * *

Sam starts the Sheriffs four-wheel drive then looks at his passengers. Sitting in the front passenger seat is Agent Adams. In the backseat sits the President, with Senator Newton sitting behind Sam.

"So, Sam...Can I call you Sam," The Presidents ask.

"Sure, I don't see why not," Sam smiles at the President while shaking his hand. As their hands touch a small spark jumps between their palms.

The Presidents feels a slight tingle, but does not give it a passing thought.

While Sam sees demons standing outside the truck, behind the President. As he releases the Presidents hand the demons vanish. His heart beats fast as he thinks he is going insane.

"It is all right Sam, the Lord is with you," Angelina reassures him.

Sam relaxes.

"Oh, and this is Senator Newton, he is part of our storm resolution committee," The President points to the Senator who smiles, nods, and then continues trying to buckle the seat belt.

"Pleasure to meet you Senator," Sam says while adjusting the rear-view-mirror, "Where to gentlemen?"

Agent Adams hands Sam a map of St. Charles County, circled on it is a wildlife sanctuary known as Bush Wildlife. The agent points to the area, "Bush Wildlife, during the Cold War our government needed a place to safely store top secret documents and other classified materiel. We chose this area because of all the unused ammo bunkers."

Sam's mind races as he remembers the box and all its contents sitting in his living room.

Outside the trucks king cab, Hebrew fights off one attack after the other as demons circle the truck then dive at him. Hebrew does manage to lean into the cab to tell Sam, "Tell them about the box. There is a great power at work here."

Sam listens to the disembodied voice then answers, "Yes, I'm familiar with all the stories…, but I always thought that part about the documents was a hoax."

"Well Sam, they aren't," the President says with a smile, "Do you think you can get us there?"

Sam bows his head, says a quick prayer then begins, "I don't think we can make it into Bush with all the snow, but don't worry you won't have to."

"Oh, and why is that," Newton asks.

"Before the snow I was in Bush Wildlife with a couple of friends...we found a box inside one of those ammo bunkers with all sorts of things related to World War Two inside of it," Sam says nervously.

The President and Newton glance at each other hardily believing their luck, "What kind of articles Sam," the President asks as Bongo and two other demons attack Hebrew.

Hebrew and Angelina take flight and yell down at Sam, "Don't worry the Lord is with you."

Sam glances out the trucks drivers' window. For a brief second he thinks he sees an angel ascending into the sky, but the vision disappears, hidden by a cloud. He turns toward the President remembering he was asked a question, "Books, little books by Henicky, a stack of manila envelops, and other interesting things don't worry, it's all sitting on a table at my house."

"Was there a red ruby among the articles," Newton asks.

"Yes, a red ruby in a red box with an eagle engraved in its lid. The ruby has a chain attached to it," Sam places the truck in gear, "Sounds like I have what you're looking for."

"Where are you going," demands Agent Adams.

"My house, it's not far," Sam says with a smile.

"Oh, leave him alone Adams," says the President, "After all, it does sound like he has what we are looking for."

Sam smiles at the President and accelerates. The truck tires spin then grip pushing the vehicle along the snow-laden road. High above a helicopter hovers carrying several dozen secret service agents. Flying along side the truck is Bongo. After several miles Sam slows the truck at the entrance to his driveway. The mountain of road sludge he climbed over is gone. A nice clean opening now exists from the main road to the house.

"Boy, Charles must have eaten all my Wheaties," Sam thinks to himself. Then he spots a man on a Bobcat sitting in his driveway. Sam pulls into the driveway stopping the truck next to him.

Sam rolls down his window, "Yeah thanks, I wasn't really looking forw…"

"Yes Sir, Mr. President. All clear just as you requested," the man on the Bobcat interrupts Sam.

The President waves two fingers at the man, "Proceed Sam," the President says calmly while looking at Sam.

"Proceed, but how did…it must have taken him hours to clear all this out…How did you know we were coming here," Sam asks sternly.

"We know many things," Newton says looking Sam in the eye.

"Yes, that is true." Agent Adams agrees.

"Yes, yes…please pull forward so we can get out of this truck and into the house. I will explain everything to you," demands the President while motioning forward with his hand.

Sam glances at all three before pulling forward then stopping next to the house. He shuts off the engine. Without saying a word they exit the vehicle and march into the house where they gather around the table in the living room. Sam enters the room last. He sees the wood near the fireplace neatly stacked and a fire blazing in the fireplace, "Charles," he calls.

"He can't hear you," Newton says grinning.

"Why, where is he," Sam asks while looking around the room.

"He is at a place called, Nicboth, along with Sharon," the Presidents says matter-of-fact like.

"And Charlotte," adds Newton.

"And Ben and Bruce," adds Agent Adams.

"Nicboth....What are you talking about," Sam asks while sitting down on the arm of the sofa.

"Well," the President begins then he sees the red box, "Oh, there it is," he picks up the box then opens it. With the tips of his fingers he lifts the chain allowing the ruby to fall free and dangle from the end of the chain.

"The Crescent," Agent Adams gasps.

"Beautiful," Newton says as he leans close to it.

"Magnificent," whispers the President as he lifts it to eye level examining its brilliance.

Sam stares at the ruby, "I bet its worth a lot of money. Is that why you wanted the box?"

"Oh, you don't understand. This is not just a ruby. It is the Crescent. The most rare and unique gem ever made," the President turns towards Sam. He walks over to him dangling the ruby in front of Sam's eyes, "This ruby is older than earth, older than the angels. Honed from a distant star and cut by a master so long ago that the stars number its age. It was a gift to God from a being no one, but God knows. It is the splendor of the universe."

Sam sits watching the ruby spin and sway, back and fourth listening to the President. Then the President yanks the ruby away.

"This ruby," the President continues, "has special powers. With it hanging around your neck a mortal like us can see the angels and demons without their help. If the angels were to use it they could see the future and past. The demons....the demons could rule the world if they new its secrets, which they don't. angels would no longer have dominion over the demon wearing the ruby and the demon wearing the ruby could kill angels."

"Where is the box," Agent Adams asks.

"Over there against the wall," Sam points.

Newton brings the trunk over to the table. He reaches inside and lifts the false bottom out of the box revealing a hidden compartment where a manila envelope lays. He hands the letter size envelope to the President.

"The Crescent is just the beginning. This," The President holds the envelope up at shoulder height looking directly at Sam, "...this is the key to unlocking the worlds riches."

Sam stares at the envelope and then at the ruby dangling carelessly from the Presidents hand. He thinks about grabbing it and making a run for it. Even at his age he feels he could out run Agent Adams, and maybe Newton. The President he isn't worried about.

The President says calmly, "No, I don't think you understand Sam. If you try what you're thinking you won't get by with it."

"How do you know what I'm thinking? Who are you," Sam asks as Agent Adams transforms into his true self, a demon called, Rae. His long thin snout projects from his skull as his eyes stretch long and thin. Wiry hair grows from his face.

Ce materializes; the President and Newton laugh.

Sam stands stepping away from them. His mind swirls in confusion not believing what his eyes behold.

"We know many things about you Sam Donaldson, alias Walter Gulf."

Sam stands defiantly looking at them wondering what to do, and then he bows his head saying a prayer. As he does, Agent Adams begins to howl as the prayer cuts through him, burning him. He runs out of the house whaling as smoke rises from his back and head.

Sam raises his head from prayer watching the agent run from the house. As Sam turns toward the President, Ce leaps at him.

***

Michlu dives at Danatallion while lunging with his sword.

Danatallion dives, spins thrusting his sword toward Michlu's abdomen.

Michlu contours, swinging his sword striking Danatallion's sword knocking it out of his hand, spins, does a back flip landing next to Danatallion pointing his sword at Danatallions neck.

Danatallion lays on the rocky soil of Nicboth breathing heavily. His eyes fixed on the sword point.

"Danatallion, surrender to God. He will figure you for all this," Michlu demands.

"Never, he is a liar," Danatallion growls then he spit's fire at Michlu.

Michlu steps to the side dodging the fireball allowing Danatallion to escape to his sword, but before he can grasp it Bel strikes him behind the neck, severing his head. Green smoke pours from the opening bellowing into the Heavens.

"It's a shame. He could have been great in Heaven," Bel says as he looks at Michlu, who is staring at the battles going on all around him then he lowers his head.

"Yes, you are right he could have been, but now will never be," Michlu says solemnly.

They hear laughter from behind them. As they turn the head of Danatallion rolls toward them, green smoke pours from its neck. The head stops a few feet away, then spins turning Danatallions face looking at them. His eyes glow a brilliant blue. Danatallion laughs, "You are fools," his voice no longer deep and billowing, but grabbled from the blood filling his throat, "As we speak my demons hold the lifeline of your precious saints. There is an hour that comes soon and they will die!" then his head withers away into a pile of dust with green smoke billowing from it.

"Ahadiel, Gethel," Michlu calls. The two angels fend off demons and dive toward Michlu.

"What is your desire, Michlu," Gethel asks as he swats a small demon off his nose.

"Our saints are in danger. Take two legions from A'albiel to assure their safety," Michlu orders.

Without hesitation the two dart skyward disappearing in the clouds.

Bel stares at Michlu then watches the puffs of green smoke in the sky from distant scrimmages rise into the Heavens, his ex-comrades, his ex-subordinates. He wants to tell them he was wrong about Que and Lucifer. They are deceivers. However, he knows they will not listen to him. They will only attack, and then he will turn them into puffs of green smoke.

Bel, recalls his battles in Heaven as he fled from God, "Lord, I will never leave you again," he says raising his hand to Heaven. In his mind he remembers the injustice served to other demons, by Que, "Michlu, I must go right a wrong," then he dashes into the sky.

Michlu watches Bel fly into the distance. He does not try to stop him because he knows where Bel is going.

* * *

A drip echoes from somewhere in the cave as the fire crackles. Sharon watches the flames dance around a few inches above the rocks. What it is burning she can't tell.

Charles is resting comfortably with his head on Charlottes lap.

Amy sits in the shadows watching.

To their left the sound of clacking rocks mixed with distant voices startles them.

"Ben, I told you, that thing grabbed me from behind. What was I suppose to do," Bruce shouts.

"You could have shouted, yelled, 'Hey Ben a big hairy dog has me,'" Ben shouts back.

"Ben, Bruce," Sharon shouts then runs toward them.

"Sharon," Ben shouts as he and Bruce run to her. They meet in the shadows and hug.

"How did you get here," Bruce asks.

"That demon brought me here," Sharon points to the two yellow eyes hovering in the darkness behind them.

Ben and Bruce turn to see the yellow eyes and begin walking toward the fire, "Us, as well," Bruce says softly as if trying to hide the fact.

"His name is Ce," Amy says laughing.

Sharon follows close behind Ben while staring at Amy.

As they reach the fire Charlotte nods and smiles. Charles looks up at Ben and Bruce, then at Sharon, "Who are they," he asks weakly.

"This is my boss, Ben…"

"Enough of these formalities," Amy shouts while staring at Ce, "Who told you to bring these two here," she sneers.

"The same one who told me to bring him," Ce growls as he points into the shadows, "…Que."

Sam walks out of the shadows joining the group.

Amy grits her teeth, "Urrrgh…Get Bel in here now! We'll settle this once and for all."

"Bel, is no longer one of us…he converted," Ce says in his low gravely voice.

"What! No way….No way," Amy shouts. Her voice echoes in the cave, "I will see to him," Amy marches away disappearing in the shadows.

"Sam," Charles shouts straining his throat, coughing violently. Charlotte holds him close.

"What happened," Sam asks as he kneels next to Charles,

small black soars raise and fall from Charles's forehead. Sam hears a wheeze with every breath Charles takes.

"That witch did this Sam. She claims Charlotte is on some kind of a mission and did this trying to force Charlotte to confess," Sharon says angrily.

Sam smiles at Charles and Charlotte, "I know your special Charlotte, but I do not think you're the one on the mission."

"No Sam, I'm not," Then she looks down at Charles and thinks to herself, "I do know who is though," she brushes the back of her hand on Charles cheek, "...and he doesn't know it."

Sam pats Charlotte's arm, then looks up at Ben and smiles, "Hi, who are you," Sam asks then returns to examining Charles.

"These are colleagues of mine, Ben Gameberlin, and Bruce Wilson. Guys this is Sam Donaldson and these two precious gems are Charles and Charlotte Hanson," they nod and say hello.

Ben steps forward and kneels next to Bruce, "How did you get here," then he stands and looks around at the group, "How did you all get here?"

"Yes," Bruce steps next to Ben, "...this cave is in the middle of the outback. Inside a mountain called Nicboth."

"Nicboth," Sharon shouts, "Here...that guy in the rain...he said, Nicboth!"

Ben pats Sharon's shoulder, "I will explain it all to you later, but tell me how you got here."

"I brought them," Ce growls as he steps out of the shadows and into the light, still beyond the flames, "...there is a higher power at work here than any of you can imagine."

"Try me, dog breath," Sharon snaps

Ce laughs, "Now, now, what would your Christ think about you getting angry, hmm."

"He turned the tables over in the temple when he found them selling goods there, didn't he," Charlotte says calmly.

"Yes, I'm sure anger is alright when used against evil," Ben says as he glares at Ce.

Ce smiles at these humans as he paces back and fourth. His four paws pat the ground rhythmically. He then stops, turning to the group, "Did your Christ not say, 'Turn the other cheek?'"

Ben starts to respond angrily then stops himself. He knows Ce is right.

"Yes," Ce continues, "...he took all the Romans threw at him. A thousand or more legends of angels at his disposal and he let them beat him then nail him to a cross, why," Ce paces staring at the group, "Because he was scared...afraid of us!"

"Get behind thee Satan. He did it to die on the cross for us! To pay for our sins, so one day we will be with him in Heaven as brothers," Charlotte shouts angrily.

"Brothers!" Ce shouts with a laugh "...then you admit it, you will be Gods. Just like him," Ce says laughing.

"No," Sam bellows, his voice echoes throughout the cavern, "There is only one God," Sam steps toward Ce who growls deep and long. Ce snarls, his eyes narrow as saliva drips from his long sharp teeth. He snaps at Sam with two quick lunges then retreats as Sam continues unhindered to the flames.

"Oh, a tough guy," Amy says laughing from the darkness.

Sam looks beyond the flames in the direction of the voice. Amy walks toward him out of the shadows still portraying herself as a young woman, "You know, Sammie," she giggles, "...your bravery is remarkable."

Sam watches Amy step into the light. Along side her is Senator Newton wearing the, Crescent, around his neck.

"Well Sam, I see you made it here in one piece," Newton smirks.

Sam stares at the, Crescent, which he knows gives Newton the ability to see all demons and angels.

Charles stares at the, emulate as well. He remembers something from an old book he read once describing such a necklace. Why this comes to mind now he doesn't know.

Newton looks at the expanse of the cave where he watches demons step from the darkness into the light of the flame. The number of demons measure into the thousands as they surround the humans.

Something stirs inside Charles pushing his memory to recall his yesterdays like they just happened. Suddenly, he feels his youthful strength return. His muscles bulge, and his hair turns a light brown. Charles feels his skin tighten. He looks up at Charlotte who looks at him and smiles saying, "Charles, it is time."

He smiles at her, and then lifts his lips to her cheek, kissing her. Charles sits up while looking at the, Crescent. "Sam," he shouts, "...the emulate is special. It contains more power than you think."

"Right you are old man," Newton laughs, "Ever since placing the chain around my neck I feel invincible."

Charles stands boldly, "No, you don't understand. It's dangerous. The power is divided; for angels its one way, for the demons another, and for humans another still," Charles steps to Sam's side and whispers, "The human who wears the, Crescent not only sees demons and angels, but also is giving immortality. Sam, you must get the Crescent from him."

"No, no Charles," Charlotte says, "You must do it. The job is assigned to you," Charlotte pats Charles hand, "Don't you worry, I'll be fine and so will you," She says with a slight smile. This is all part of a premonition she had long ago when an angel told her, "One day, Charles will glorify God by beating a snake. Then soon after, both of you will walk together in paradise." She bows her head saying a quick pray. Then she steps close to Sharon holding her hand. Ben and Bruce step close to them.

Simon, a demon whose hatred for humans pales in comparison to his hatred toward angels stands behind Bruce. His blunt snoot hovers inches above Bruce's shoulder.

"Do you smell that," Bruce asks Ben softly.

"Yeah, it smells like rotten eggs," Ben wrinkles his nose sniffing the air, "It's coming from you," Ben whispers.

"Me," Bruce blurts out, then collects himself, "That isn't funny."

Charles looks at Newton and Amy then steps beyond the fire standing bravely a few yards before them. He points his finger at Newton, "I do not know who you are, but your toying in a realm you know nothing about!"

"Oh, I know plenty. Probably more than you will ever understand." Newton says with a chuckle.

"What is your name," Charles asks while stepping closer.

Ce snarls.

"Newton, his name is Senator Newton," Sam responds while glaring into Newton's eyes.

"Newton," Ben whispers then digs into his pocket pulling out the tie clip. He holds it up showing Bruce, "Remember, we found this over there."

Bruce stares at the clip, then asks softly, "Do you think that belongs to him?"

"Why of course it does. When we get out of here we will go straight to the press," Ben says in a whisper.

"Yeah, if we get out of here," Bruce says while watching Newton storm toward them.

Newton marches to Ben holding out his hand, "You have something that belongs to me, hand it over...Now!"

Ben shoves the clip back into his pocket, "Why should I?"

Newton reaches out to grab Bens arm when Sam grabs Newton's shoulder from behind turning Newton around, punching him in the nose. Newton falls to the rocky ground.

"See," shouts Sam, "You bleed…you're still human!"

Newton wipes the blood from his nose with the back of his hand.

"Yes, bravo," Amy yells while clapping, "I love this…do it again," she trots up to Sam, "Go ahead, do it again. That was marvelous," she demands with a smile.

Sharon steps close to Amy, "I wonder if you bleed as well," Sharon punches Amy across the jaw.

Amy stands still for a moment then turns her head slowly toward Sharon.

Sharon slowly steps backward; her punch had no effect on Amy.

Amy's face transforms to her natural look, a wolf. She snarls at Sharon with salvia dripping off her fangs.

Sharon stares into Amy's eyes, then trips over rocks, falling to the ground near the fire.

Amy steps toward her.

Charles rushes to Sharon kneeling next to her, then shouting at Amy, "You have no power over her."

Amy steps back hissing at them.

Sam turns toward Amy, marching toward her.

Newton stands and begins running toward Sam.

Ben and Bruce reach out to grab Newton as Charlotte grabs the Crescent, breaking the chain from around Newton's neck.

Newton turns, glaring at Charlotte.

Amy reaches her hand into the air, before turning toward Charlotte, "Anay eplotis neumon," she shouts then squeezes her hand into a tight fist.

Charlotte drops the, Crescent as she collapse to the ground.

Sam punches Amy in the back of the head sending her stumbling forward.

Newton swings a wild left at Sam as Charles punches him in the stomach, doubling Newton over where he falls to the ground.

Bruce picks up the Crescent and immediately sees all the demons around him.

Simon bends down low to stare directly into Bruce's eyes, "If you can see me then I can hurt you!" Simon sneers.

Bruce faints, dropping the Crescent. Ben picks up the Crescent and beholds the demons around him, "Crap!"

Amy turns toward Sam hissing loud and long.

Charles rushes to Charlotte's side passing dangerously close to Amy who is stepping toward Sam.

"Come on," Sam shouts.

As Amy approaches Sam, the ground begins to tremble violently. Stalactites drop from the caves ceiling shattering on the cave's floor.

Amy staggers then she falls to the ground.

Ben grabs Bruce's arm to balance himself. The Crescent dangles from his fist. The ability to see the demons passes through Ben to Bruce which allows both of them to watch the demons run through the far tunnel toward Nicboth's surface fleeing the shacking cavern.

Charles lies across Charlotte protecting her from rock debris flying through the air from crashing stalactites.

Sam stands next to Sharon as the ground beneath them lurches upward then suddenly drops only to begin rocking from side to side. The cavern floor cracks and splits into fissures spewing hot red magma onto the cave floor. The cavern glows red as the fissure widen.

Red lines crisscross in front of Newton as he tries to stand. He looses his balance falling into a fissure disappearing into the red glow.

Ben falls to the ground. He loses his grip dropping the Crescent next to a pile of rocks that glow as red as the ruby. As he reaches for the chain a fissure opens, then widens separating

Bruce and Ben from the ruby. They watch helplessly as the fissure widens.

Charles looks up from taking Charlottes pulse. There is none. She is dead. Hebrew kneels next to Charles, "Charlotte is in a better place, come we have work to do. Charles turns his tear-filled eyes toward the voice to see Hebrew dressed in white wearing a gold rope around his waist. He shines brighter than anything he has ever seen before. A peace falls over him.

"Yes, what is it you want me to do?"

"Take the Crescent to God. It must be delivered by you," Hebrew instructs.

"Why can't you deliver it," Charles asks as a fissure explodes nearby sending magma flying into the air. Small fireballs of magma splash at Charles's feet, but he does not notice.

"If an angel touches it they will fall from grace as they will know the future and the past. Their being chances from an angel to a demon," Hebrew says as he points to it, "It is wonderful to behold, but dangerous to hold. Take it Charles....take it to God."

"Yes, I will," Charles, shouts as he steps past Hebrew toward the edge of the fissure. The ground sways, then shakes, lifts then drops sending Charles to his knees unable to stand. He looks around for Hebrew, but he is gone.

"Charles," Sharon shouts, "This way! The fissure is cutting you off. Get out of there!" Sharon yells.

Sam, Ben and Bruce all yell for him to hurry as the fissure finishes its circle completely cutting off Charles escape. He stands looking at them then at the Crescent. He smiles and waves. He knows he will never be with them again.

The small circle of the cave floor becomes an island floating in the midst of a red river of magma. Charles watches as the island slowly shrinks, melting away by the heat. It will only be a matter of time before the island, the ruby, and he will no longer exist. The heat around him chokes him; he struggles for every morsel of air. As he breaths in the hot air it burns his throat and lungs. Closing his eyes he prays.

"Don't give up Charles," Charles listens to Charlotte's voice. He opens his eyes to see her body still lying motionless, "The Crescent Charles, take it!"

"It will melt with the island," Charles struggles to speak, "I haven't the strength, may God forgive me."

He turns his gaze to the Crescent where Ce stands glaring at him. Ce's body silhouettes against the intense heat behind him. His yellow eyes glow with bright intensity.

"You," Ce snarls, "I will tear you apart."

Charles heart leaps as a sudden calm overwhelms him; a renewed strength enters his heart and soul. He once again stands boldly as before fearing only God.

"No," Charles says sternly looking into the yellow embers of Ce's eyes, "...you are the one that will be torn apart."

Ce growls then turns with a flash grabbing the Crescent, "You have no rule over me! I am immortal," Ce begins to leap across the red lake of fire to the cave floor when he is stopped in mid leap.

Charles has him by the tail, "No, I don't think so," Charles pulls Ce back with a jerk causing Ce to drop the Crescent at the islands edge. Charles spins Ce around tossing him into the lava. The cave fills with the agonizing howls of Ce as the magma devours him.

Charles picks up the ruby then steps back as the island rapidly dissolves before him. He watches Charlottes lifeless bodily ignite then roll into the red river. He stands in the middle of the island, crosses his arms across his chest then slowly sinks into the red mass.

"Charles," Sharon shrieks stepping toward the river of magma. Sam garbs her by the shoulders pulling her back.

"It's alright Sharon, it's alright," Sam says as he holds her tight.

"Come on, we have to go and go quick," Ben shouts while pointing toward a large mass of magma rolling toward them. The four turn and run with Ben leading the way to the tunnel.

"This way," Ben shouts, "The tunnel is our only way out," Ben stops at the mouth of the tunnel, "Come on, hurry!"

Bruce, Sharon, and Sam hurry through the tunnel opening with Ben close behind. They do not slow down until they reach the low part of the tunnel where Ben had placed a large, X, the day before. They sit, breathing heavily and resting.

"The tunnels ceiling is pretty low here. Sharon you might not have to much of a problem, but Sam…Sam you will have to crouch." Ben informs them as Bruce nods in approval.

"This won't be easy, Sam, but if I can do it then you can," Bruce encourages Sam as he takes a bottle of water out of his backpack handing it to Sharon. She takes a drink and passes it to Sam. Ben pours some over his face.

"Come on lets get going. I don't know about you guys, but the faster we get out of here the faster I'm going to feel better," Sharon says as she stands.

"Yep, I'll drink to that," Bruce says with a smile.

Chapter 11
Ascension

The sun shines bright as the four exit the tunnel squinting their eyes. Sam and Bruce arch their backs then stretch after their long hike where they walked bent over. Sharon stands gazing up the fifty-foot flint rock slope along side Ben.

"When we came down we used this rope to lower ourselves. We can use it to pull ourselves up," Ben tugs on the rope reassuring himself that the line holds firm at the other end.

"I'll go first then I can help pull you guys up." Sam suggests.

As he climbs the flint rock slides beneath his boots sending clouds of dust swelling up around him. The rocks clatter together echoing in the small crevasse.

Bruce leans against the tunnel entrance watching Sam when he hears cackling coming from the tunnel.

"Ben, do you hear anything," Bruce asks as he looks down the tunnel.

"No, all I hear is rocks clattering together. What do you hear?"

"Oh, nothing I suppose. Sounded like cackling," Bruce says stepping toward the rope.

"Cackling," Sharon questions Bruce as she watches him pick up the end of the rope. She steps to the tunnel entrance and listens. She hears something faint, a vague noise, almost like a laugh, "Shhh" she waves toward Ben.

"Sam, stop! I think Sharon hears something too." Ben looks over at Sharon as Sam stands still. Bruce holds the rope with both hands.

Sharon lens toward the opening listening, "Yes, it is cackling," She yells, "Hurry, get up that slope," Sam digs his heels in pulling the rope as he climbs to the top.

Bruce, already ten feet up the slope isn't waiting for Sam to finish.

Ben helps Sharon to the rope, starting her on her way. Then he picks up a dried tree limb to use as a club.

Sharon looks behind her, "Ben come on, you can't stop them!"

"No, but I might slow them down," Ben shouts, "Now get going!"

Sam reaches the top then turns helping Bruce up. Sharon is not far behind Bruce, "Dog gone it Ben, lets go," Sam shouts.

Ben looks up the slope seeing Sharon at the top. He drops the club and grabs the rope, beginning his ascent. The rocks slide beneath his boots as he struggles up the embankment. As he nears the top demons explode from the tunnel entrance.

Like bats small demons known as Dadters, rocket out of the tunnel swarming in large groups high above. These demons have long fangs and claws capable of ripping a human in half. The swarm grows larger as they gather high above.

Sam grabs Bens arm pulling him over the top.

"Let get out of here, Sam, follow me," Ben shouts.

The group squeezes through the narrow opening between two

boulders then run haphazardly down a dusty slope, past the egg shaped boulder, to the Aborigine's temple.

As they enter the temple the demons dive down swarming around them. The four huddle close together as around them fly the Dadters, cackling loudly.

"What are they," Sharon shouts covering her ears as the cackling is deafening.

Suddenly, the Dadters fly upward, hovering high above. Over the rocky ridge of the temple a dark cloud swirls, rolling toward them. Like smoke pouring from a furnace, the cloud folds, rolls and grows as it approaches. It stops its approach in the center of the temple, where it grows larger while rolling and pulsating. It begins to spin, swirling faster until it burst, exploding in all directions. As the cloud dissipates Que appears.

On the side of Que's head grow ram horns, his teeth are black as night; his face pale as death; his eyes, nose, and mouth outlined in red. His body is the body of a snake, with rear goat's legs and hoofs. His arms are Herculaneum, with large muscles and strong forearms. He stands over the group as if they were children. His stature large and imposing looms down on the group gripping them in fear.

"Where are you going," Que asks as he walks around them.

"In the name of Christ, be gone from here," Sam shouts.

"I will, but I will take all of you with me," Que raises his hand above his head, "Take them," he orders his Dadters.

The demons swoop down out of the sky like locust trapping the group within a black spiral.

The group stands with their back to one another watching helplessly. The cackling throng spins around them in an ever-increasing flurry. Slowly the circle grows smaller. The Dadters ready their claws and fangs.

A black billowing cloud emerges on the far horizon rolling

toward the temple. Directly over the spinning caldron it turns inside out throwing a fist in the form of a cloud downward where it strikes the Dadters with a thunderous explosion of water casting them in all directions. Some die instantly exploding in green puffs of smoke, while others strike rocks or each other then explode with their green essence lofting skyward. Most flutter off into surrounding hillsides wanting no more of the cloud.

Bel, is the first to fly out of the dark cloud. He raises his sword diving at Que. Lightning flashes as thunder erupts. A wall of water pours from the dark expanse encompassing the entire temple grounds.

Sharon, Sam, Ben, and Bruce run to the edge of the temple under a rock outcrop watching Bel as he slashes at Que. Their swords clash sending sparks exploding all around them. Sharon watches closely, but something catches her eye. Walking in the wall of water is someone dressed as a Roman solider.

"Look," she shouts above the pouring rain.

"I don't believe it...it...its Norwick," Ben yells.

Norwick walks steadily toward Que with his empty sheath dangling from his belt, bouncing off his thigh. As he approaches Bel pulls back allowing Norwick free rein to speak.

"Que," Norwick shouts, "Lift my imprisonment, set me free!"

Que turns his gaze from Bel to Norwick who stands defiant.

"Be gone from here little man. Neither you nor the rebel Bel have power over me," Que says laughing.

"But I do," thunders a voice from above. Michlu lowers slowly from the sky to land along side Norwick, "I have the power given by God to defeat you."

"You're pathetic Michlu, we were created at the same time, twins. That 'God' of yours made us together. You have no more power against me than I do over you."

"I choose to stay with him and you rebelled forfeiting your rights. I do have dominion here?"

"Prove it," Que swats at Michlu causing Norwick and Michlu to dive out of the way. The large sword lands flat in the muddy soil splattering mud everywhere.

Michlu takes flight diving alongside Bel toward Que.

Norwick holds his arms in the air summoning all his might to the cloud directing the wall of water onto Que.

Michlu and Bel divide their attack diving from opposite sides.

As they reach Que they dodge Que's sword then slash Que across his shoulders. This has no effect as Que continues fighting relentlessly. His sword swings from side to side holding Michlu and Bel at bay.

Sam, looks across the temple grounds seeing someone walking toward them, it's Charles.

"Charles," Sam yells.

"Charles," Sharon yells. She runs out to him, wrapping her arms around his neck almost knocking him over, "How, why…Oh your alive!"

"Well, now hold on there," Charles smiles, "Yes, I do have the Crescent you know, that makes me immortal."

Ben, Sam, and Bruce join them all shaking his hand.

"I know you're all wondering how, but this is not the time or place. I have work to do, then I have a date with a good looking blonde," Charles smiles, turns his back to them, then walks toward Que.

Sam then remembers Charlottes words, "One day, Charles will glorify God by beating a snake. Then soon after, both of you will walk together in paradise," Sam understands and tells the others what he remembers, "Charles is doing what Charles must do," he adds.

Charles marches straight to Que, "Que," Charles shouts.

Que looks down at Charles.

Michlu and Bel pull back their attacks while Norwick redirects the wall away from Charles.

"What do you want with me little man," Que's voice thunders.

"Your death or surrender will do nicely, I suppose," Charles says sheepishly as he looks up at Que.

Que laughs, "Death, surrender? You're giving me a choice?"

"Not exactly, you're death I suppose would be nice, but I prefer your surrender," Charles turns toward the sky, "Oh Lord, let your will be done," as the words leave his lips a sword falls at his feet.

"Here, use that one. Norwick doesn't need it," Que laughs.

Charles picks up the sword tossing it to Norwick.

Norwick smiles as he holds his sword. He feels completely again.

"I don't need a sword," Charles says looking up at Que walking towards him.

Que laughs, then looks up as Michlu and Bel diving toward him. As Que prepares to defend himself Charles stands next to his tail.

Charles says a short prayer, then places his hand on the tail. The moment he touches it the skin transforms to stone spreading all over Que. Charles walks away toward the group.

Que raises his sword to block a plunge by Bel when his arm remains fixed in place.

"What is this…I can't move," the paralysis moves up Que's body to his neck. His eyes fixed, staring directly at a cloud that swirls and transforms into the face that glows brighter than the sun.

"All I ask is your surrender, Que. Ask forgiveness and I will set you free," the voice echoes out of the cloud.

Que can barely move his lips, "Nev….Never," he squeaks

then his lips turn to stone. His entire being stands looming above the temple.

Sam steps from under the overhang looking up at this huge statue.

"Wow," Sharon gasps as she stands next to Ben and Bruce looking up at Que.

Bruce leans over to Ben, "Is he…dead?"

"Well…I don't know," Ben says rubbing his chin looking up at the gray stone figure.

Michlu and Bel land nearby then walk over to the group.

"He is no harm now," Bel says as he pats Bruce on the back.

Bruce looks up at Bel and smiles, "Thanks, for saving us!"

"Oh, it was Michlu who talked me into coming here. Norwick and I were going to go to Nicboth," Bel explains as he looks around, "There, there is Norwick."

Across the temple grounds walks Norwick toward them. With Que's power gone the rain no longer imprisons him.

"Thank you old friend for remembering me," Norwick shakes Bel's hand then hugs him. Michlu steps near and they all three hug and shout, "Glory to God in the highest!"

Ben then walks over to Norwick, "I don't know if you remember me. I…"

Norwick interrupts, "Why yes I do. The Congo, right?"

"Yes," Ben says laughing, "You do remember me, and I wanted to thank you for saving me from those head hunters."

"My pleasure," Norwick says smiling, then reaches down touching Bens hip. Immediately Bens hip socket rejuvenates, becoming whole again.

"Glory be," Ben shouts!

Michlu then steps away from the group then turns facing them, "Sharon, Ben, Bruce, and Sam, thank you for not running when the going became tough. Thank you for having faith! The Lord watches and talks to the Father concerning you four."

"But what about Charlotte, and Charles," Bruce asks sternly.

"Oh, don't worry about us," Charles says walking up behind Bruce, "You do remember I told you I have a date with a good looking blonde, well there she is!"

Charles points to a cloud and there on the cloud sits Charlotte as young and youthful as ever. She waves to them and they wave up to her, "Before I can be with her I have to give this to its rightful owner," Charles holds up the Crescent.

"Good for you Charles," Sharon says smiling.

"Whelp, any time your ready, Michlu, I'm ready," Charles says as he steps to Michlu's side.

Michlu smiles as he touch's Charles's shoulder. They both slowly rise with Bel and Norwick along side.

At first Charles is nervous, but then waves smiling as the excitement of going to Heaven overcomes his fear of heights, "You guys don't take forever now, and I'll be waiting for ya!"

"Bye," shouts Ben and Bruce.

"See ya," waves Sam.

"We'll miss you both," Shouts Sharon

The four stand watching as the angels and Charles ascend high into the sky.

"Whelp, I guess that's it, but I do have a question Ben," Bruce asks as the four walk along the trail.

Ben looks over at Bruce unsure if he wants to answer anymore of Bruce's question, then decides why not, "Go ahead Bruce, you asks anything you want. I'm sure between the three of us we can figure out the answer."

"Good, was it the angels or demons that wanted us to go to Nicboth," Bruce asks quizzically then stops waiting for the answer.

Ben smiles at him. Right away Bruce knows the answer before Ben replies, "Both."

"Now Ben, that is you usual pat answer…how can you….errrr."

The four laugh as they round a bend in the trail.

End